LOST IN ME

Here and Now series, book one

LOST IN ME

Here and Now series, book one

LEXI RYAN

For Adrienne. Here's to writing dates, laughter, and dreams brought to life.

PROLOGUE

September—Eleven Months Before Accident

WHEN MAXIMILIAN Hallowell winks at me, my heart somersaults like an overzealous toddler at her first gymnastics class. Because, yes, when it comes to this guy, I am so over-the-top awkward that even the metaphorical tumbling of my internal organs is cringe-worthy.

I force myself to return his smile, but his attention has already shifted to my twin. My so-obviously-not-identical-it's-laughable twin.

"Go finish your drinks," Lizzy says, shooing the guys toward their table. "We need some time for girl talk."

I wish she wouldn't do that. Even if he hardly knows I exist, I want to be close to Max. When he's near, I forget how to breathe, yet I feel more alive than ever.

Lizzy slides into our booth and tugs me in beside her as Cally takes a seat across from us.

"What's that about?" Cally asks me, concern pulling on her features.

I shake my head. I should be glad Lizzy sent Max away. I'm so transparent. I probably would've made a fool of myself.

"She's got a crush on Max," Lizzy explains.

I jab my elbow into Lizzy's side—my crush on the unattainable Maximilian Hallowell is not for public consumption.

Lizzy ignores me. "Can't say as I blame her. You could bounce quarters off the boy's ass."

"He has no idea I exist," I whisper to Cally. "He's only had eyes for Lizzy since he came back to town and opened that gym."

Lizzy frowns, and I feel guilty for bringing it up. "I never would have gone on that date with him if I'd known Hanna liked him. I dropped him the minute I found out."

"Does he know how you feel?" Cally asks me.

"God, no!" Lizzy says before I can reply. "Are you kidding? Hanna doesn't tell guys when she's interested. She'd rather hide and believe she doesn't stand a chance. Which is stupid and a lie."

I shoot a conspicuous glance toward the guys' table just to make sure Max isn't listening in on this conversation. *Like he cares.* "What would he want to do with me anyway?" I mutter. "He's an athletic trainer who runs his own health club, and I'm a fat girl."

"Hanna!" Lizzy and Cally screech in unison.

I regret the F-word as soon as it leaves my lips. There are unspoken rules to being the chubby chick in a group of friends, and *numero uno* is that you never use the F-word. I can't do anything but shrug. The rule can't be unbroken. The ugly truth is out there. "Sorry."

"You're fucking gorgeous, and any guy would be lucky to have you." Lizzy gets so pissed off when I dare suggest her long, lithe limbs are more desirable than my size sixteen-to-eighteen "curves" ("curves" being the PC word for "extra layers of fat"). Reality doesn't even enter into her perception of the situation. Reality is that I've had a handful of dates that were terrible and two boyfriends who were even worse. Lizzy, on the other hand, has her pick of the lot. Including Max Hallowell.

There's honestly not enough beer in that pitcher for me to

deal with this conversation tonight. "Time to change the subject, please."

Lizzy presses a kiss to my forehead and whispers so only I can hear, "My Hanna wants Max, my Hanna's gonna get Max."

Chapter
ONE

STORIES AREN'T supposed to start with the main character waking up. It's a rule I learned in my creative writing class in college. Something about boring the reader or being a cliché or… Actually, I don't remember the reason.

But dreams? A lot of my dreams start with me waking up, and this is too surreal to be anything but a dream. Opening my eyes, I find myself in the hospital, not knowing how or why, the nurse telling me that I've been here for over twenty-four hours.

"Mother's maiden name?" a nurse is asking me. She's been quizzing me for several minutes now. My name, my birthday, the freaking president of the United States.

I blink against the fluorescent overhead lights and supply, "Crossen." My head hurts like a thousand drunken clowns have been dancing on it. In cleats.

"Do you know the date?"

I grimace as I shift on the hospital mattress, and the movement sends pain ricocheting through muscles I didn't even know I had. I'm sure she has a good reason for these questions, but I'd like to ask some of my own, starting with, *Why am I in the hospital?* And, *Who beat the shit out of me?*

"September…twelfth, maybe? Thirteenth?" The words come

out more like croaks than coherent syllables and they feel like a cheese grater against my throat.

"August," someone squeaks behind her. "She means August. Don't you, Hanna?"

Lizzy comes into my line of sight. Her blond curls bounce as she nods at me, as if it's *really* important that I agree with her. Of course, she's completely wrong. It's not August. It's September. We're a month into the fall semester of our senior year at Sinclair.

I try to frown but it hurts. My hand flies to my face, where the pain radiates like a mini explosion. I touch my cheek gingerly and wince.

Machines beep around my head, and even though I know I just woke up, all I really want is to take some good drugs for this headache and have a nap. "Why am I in the hospital? What happened?"

"Do you know who this is, Hanna?" The nurse motions to her right.

I roll my head to the side so I can more easily focus on my sister. Her curly blond hair frames her face at awkward angles, as if she's been sleeping on a park bench or something.

I'm trying not to panic, but again, I just woke up in a hospital, I don't know how I got here, they say I've been here for over a day, and they're asking if I know my name. My face feels like it's been introduced to a set of brass knuckles, and my skull is threatening to explode. These are not generally signs of a quiet night in.

Lizzy's eyes are red. She's been crying. I keep thinking of that second pitcher of beer we ordered at Brady's. Did we drink and drive? Lizzy looks well but really upset. Is someone hurt?

"Lizzy," I ask, "what happened?"

"She knows me, see?" Lizzy says. "She's fine."

"Can you tell me how Lizzy is related to you?" the nurse asks.

"She's my twin sister."

"Good," the nurse coos. "Good job. And can you tell me the last thing you remember?"

I don't have long to consider her question before she's invading my personal bubble, her face too close to mine as she stares into my eyes. What? Did she lose something in there she's looking to get back?

"We were at Brady's. Girls' night. What happened?" God, I sound like a broken record.

"You've had an accident," the woman says, looking to my sister, who's shaking her head. A tear slips from the corner of Lizzy's eye. "A rough fall down some stairs. Can you tell me the last thing you remember before Brady's?"

"I was finishing up a paper for school. All the days blur together during the semester. I don't...I don't know."

"The semester?" Lizzy cries. "What are you talking about, Hanna?" She turns to the nurse. "I thought you said she'd be better once she was lucid?"

"It's okay," the woman assures her. "You're going to upset her."

"What happened at Brady's?" Lizzy asks me. "What do you remember?"

"We were hanging out with Cally, and the guys were there and they came over to join us."

"What were we talking about?" Lizzy presses.

She seems distressed, so I try to smile. That's my job, after all. I'm the one who makes things better. "We were trying to convince Cally that she should sleep with William."

"That happened *last September*," Lizzy whispers.

The nurse's brow creases. "Dr. Reid is on her rounds now. I'll update her, and she'll be in shortly."

Lizzy watches the woman leave then turns back to me. "Don't worry. Nix's going to fix you right up."

"Who's Nix?" I whisper.

Tears fill her eyes. "Our friend Nix. You know, Dr. Reid. She moved to town last winter?"

"I don't know any doctors named Nix, Liz."

Before she can explain herself, a pretty young woman enters in a dark dress and a white lab coat. She has long chestnut hair pulled off her neck in a twist and a warm smile. "I hear you're doing much better than last time I saw you."

I look to Liz, hoping she'll help me out.

"Do you remember her now?" my sister asks me.

I frown at the woman I'm supposed to know and shake my

head. "I'm sorry."

"My name is Dr. Phoenix Reid. You call me Nix."

The nurse reenters the room and hands a clipboard to Nix, who scans it and nods.

"Why doesn't she remember you?" Liz asks the doctor.

Nix gives her a stern look. "Calm down. Hanna, do you remember anything else after your night at the bar?"

I shake my head, panic rising. "You guys are freaking me out. What happened? Did I drink too much?"

"You've had a head injury," Nix says, "and sometimes with head injuries you can experience a degree of amnesia."

"She doesn't have *amnesia*," Lizzy objects.

"There are different kinds of amnesia. There is no need to panic."

The room grows cold all of the sudden, and I'm overwhelmed with that anxious, claustrophobic feeling I've always gotten when I feel helpless and out of control. "Is this some kind of a joke?"

"She's awake? Talking?" The deep, familiar voice rips my attention away from Dr. Reid and to the other side of the room, where Max Hallowell is bursting through the door, worry creasing his gorgeous face as his eyes roam over me in my no-dignity hospital gown.

Not that my day was going great before this moment, what with the drunken, cleated clowns dancing inside my skull, and amnesia diagnosis and all, but Max Hallowell seeing me in this condition—and *especially* in this gown—sends my day from shitty to *you've-got-to-be-effing-kidding-me*.

"I'm sorry, sir," the nurse says. "Immediate family only. You need to leave."

Ignoring her, he rushes over to my bed and rests his big hand gently against my face. The feel of his rough palm against the skin of my cheek has my heart pounding fast and hard. *Max* is touching me.

This is definitely a dream.

"Sir!" the nurse scolds.

"I am her family," he bites out.

"It's okay," Nix tells the nurse.

Max's gaze drifts to my hand and he adds, "I'm her fiancé."

I draw in my breath so hard and fast that my bruised ribs wail against my expanded lungs. Then I see what he was looking at. The fat diamond winks up at me from my ring finger as if it knows all my secrets. My world is spinning. This all has to be some kind of elaborate joke, and I don't think it's funny at all.

"Baby," he whispers. "Do you remember yet? What happened?"

"She doesn't remember," Lizzy says, her voice cold.

I feel like everyone is twenty steps ahead of me. "Fiancé?"

"Hanna has a case of retrograde amnesia," Nix tells Max. "This can happen with head injuries."

"But it's not like *normal* amnesia," Lizzy objects. "She knows who she is. She knows who *I* am."

"Her most recent memory seems to be of a night in September," the doctor says patiently. "Retrograde amnesia isn't the same as global amnesia. Likely, her memory of everything before that point is just fine. That's why she remembers Lizzy and you, who she's always known, but doesn't remember me, since we just met in December."

"She lost only *part* of her memory?" Liz asks. "Will it come back?"

I'm too busy looking at the ring. A ring from *Max*. How could I forget that?

"There's a strong possibility most of her memory of the months in between will come back. Possibly in hours, but it could take up to a few weeks or months."

The blood drains from Max's face and his Adam's apple bobs as he swallows. "Last September?"

"*Most* of her memory?" Lizzy asks. "She won't remember everything?"

I can't pretend to understand the emotions going over Max's face. Honestly, I don't know him that well. Or…do I? I shake my head, trying to focus as Nix explains my condition to Max and Liz. *Retrograde amnesia. Don't know when or if my memories will come back. Spontaneous recovery is likely. Little by little but not all at once. Timeline is different for every patient.*

"You remember Max, don't you, Hanna?" Lizzy is asking. She's moved closer to my bed now too. It's starting to feel crowded in here. Too many people and these things they're saying that don't make any sense.

"Of course I remember Max," I mutter. "We all grew up together."

"Do you remember this?" He picks up my hand and rubs his thumb over my finger. "Do you remember me giving it to you?"

"Yeah," Lizzy says. "When did that happen anyway? Was anyone going to bother to tell me my *twin sister* is getting married?"

I can barely process Lizzy's frustrated questions. I'm too focused on retrieving a memory of this ring. Max down on one knee, music, candlelight, anything. But the ring is as meaningful to me as the doctor who says I call her Nix. "I…I want to remember."

He closes his eyes, shielding them from me as his broad chest rises and falls on a deep breath.

"We'll need to run some tests," Nix says. "But the best thing you can do for Hanna is give her time. She needs rest and support right now. Not stress."

"We'll help you remember, Han-Han," Lizzy says.

"It doesn't work like that." Nix moves to the computer in the corner and types something in. "But tell her whatever she needs to return to living her life. Those memories might be back before you know it."

"Cally and Maggie are in the waiting room," Lizzy says. "I'm going to run out and give them an update. Can I get you anything?"

A healthy memory? Evidence that this isn't all just some bizarre dream? "No. I'm fine. Thanks."

Lizzy leaves, and exhaustion sweeps over me. My eyelids are heavy and my thoughts muddy with the implications of everything I've learned in the last fifteen minutes.

"When do I get to go home?" I ask in a whisper.

The doctor taps at the keyboard a few more times before turning to me. "Not today and probably not tomorrow. We need to run the tests and observe you for the next twenty-four to thirty-six hours. If everything goes as well as can be expected, you can go home after that."

Max takes my hand between his two warm ones.

Nix checks the display panel on the tower connected to my IV and presses a few buttons. "Let the nurses know if you need anything. Unfortunately, because of the head injury, we can't give you much for the pain other than Tylenol and ibuprofen, but try to sleep as much as you can. I'll see you on my rounds tomorrow." She flips off the lights at the door. "Rest. Take good care of her, Max. You know how to reach me."

I sleep fitfully, the pain in my head and ribs keeping me from settling into my dreams. When the early morning sun peeks in between the curtains, Max is still in the chair next to my bed. He's slumped over, sleeping, his dark hair falling into his face. I want to reach out and brush it back.

I try to roll to my side, but the movement puts pressure on my ribs and sends a jolt of pain through my center. I bite back my cry, but not before it wakes Max. He hops out of his chair and comes to stand by my side.

"Are you okay? What hurts?"

Eyes closed, I focus on my breathing. Inhaling. Exhaling.

"Do you want me to call the nurse? They can give you something else for the pain." His face is etched with worry as he scans mine.

"I'm okay," I assure him, because I know they can't give me anything else. "I'm just a little banged up."

"Okay." He lets out a breath and drags his hand through his hair. "This has been hell, you know. The last couple of days. You couldn't even carry on a conversation. They'd ask you one question, and by the time you answered it, you'd be confused all over again. I thought…" He shakes his head. "I didn't know if I'd ever get you back."

I have to swallow the thickness in my throat. "I'm here now."

After dragging the chair another foot closer to the bed, he sits and takes my hand. He toys with the ring on my finger, and a smile plays at his lips. "I like seeing this on you."

"You gave me this ring?" I whisper.

He lifts my hand and presses a gentle kiss to my knuckle right above the diamond. "I did."

"Why? I mean…how? I mean…" I bite my lip. My stomach is a mess of nerves.

He tucks a lock of hair behind my ear and gives a sad smile, his fingers working tiny circles on my palm. "How? I'm just a lucky bastard, I guess."

"Hmm." I rest my head back on my pillow and relax. "Sounds like it. Lucky guy is engaged to a girl who has a beat-up face and can't even remember dating him."

"Surely I can work this to my advantage." His eyes crinkle in the corners with his smile. He is so damn handsome. "Let me remind you all the ways I was the world's greatest boyfriend. The flowers, the foot massages, the…what else?"

"Coach bags," I supply. "The many Coach bags you bought me during our courtship."

"I'll admit, I never bought you a Coach bag."

I scoff. "And I accepted your proposal?"

"I love you, Hanna," he says softly, and more surprising than the words is this feeling in my chest. As if something there knows what he says is true, even if my mind can't remember how we got here.

"I…" What am I supposed to say? To echo the words back to him would ring empty. We both know I don't remember being with him, let alone falling in love. *I'm sure I love you too?* That option seems like a kick in the pants.

"It's okay," he murmurs, kissing my hand again. "I know you don't remember. I'll win your heart all over again if I have to."

Chapter
TWO

I OPEN MY eyes to see my sister Maggie's head bobbing to music I can faintly make out from her headphones, her gaze focused on the print-filled pages of a thick textbook.

"So what else do I not remember?" I ask groggily. "Are you having Asher's babies yet?"

She lifts her head and grins at me as she pulls off her headphones. "Hey, how'd you sleep?"

"Like a baby. In the literal awake-every-two-hours sense of the cliché." Hospitals have to be the worst places to get rest. Every time I would fall asleep, the nurse would come in to check something or change an IV bag. I tap Maggie's book. "What are you studying?"

"I'm doing an independent study in women in art history. Trying to catch up and make up for the year I took off."

"So that's a no on the babies?"

"Unless you count Zoe, no. No babies."

I nod thoughtfully. I remember Zoe. She's Asher's daughter who lives in New York. She spent most of the summer here—well, last summer at least. This gap in my memories is so bizarre. Not like forgetting what you did last weekend when you know time passed but just can't pin down any memories, but like the last year never happened.

I roll carefully to my side, mindful of my bruised ribs. No breaks, the doctor informed me. Just nasty bruises. Lucky me. Between tests and sleeping and being prodded by the nurses, I haven't gotten many answers to my questions.

"What happened to me, Maggie?"

"We don't really know." She closes the book and sets it to the side. "Lizzy found you at the bottom of the stairs behind the bakery. You were unconscious and looked, well"—she winces—"actually a sight better than you do now. Those bruises have gotten colorful."

"What bakery?"

"Your bakery." A slow grin lights her face. "You opened a bakery."

"I did? Mom didn't flip out?" I've always loved baking, much to the dismay of my fat-phobic mother.

She shrugs. "I don't know, but you wanted to do it and you did. It's downtown and does a nice little business. And your wedding cakes are gorgeous."

"My wedding cakes?" I've decorated cakes for friends' birthdays for years and always loved to play with frosting, gum paste, and fondant. I watched wedding cake shows on TV obsessively. But it was just a dream. Nothing I ever believed I'd be able to make a career out of.

She smiles. "We're all so proud of you."

"So then I have a bakery and I mysteriously ended up bruised and battered behind it."

"Our best guess is that you took a pretty good fall down the stairs."

I narrow my eyes at her. "So you're saying I didn't find gracefulness in those months I can't remember?"

She chuckles. "You're a hell of a lot more graceful than I am."

"What else did I miss?"

"You didn't miss anything," she says. "You were here for all of it, and that memory's going to be back in no time. I'm sure of it."

"Humor me."

"You and Liz graduated in May."

I lift my hand and study my ring. "And then there's me and Max."

"Yeah. Since, I don't know, maybe December or so? But the engagement is new. In fact, that's been a surprise to all of us. Mom came by while you were sleeping last night and she practically bawled when Max confirmed that the ring on your finger was from him and it was the real deal."

"Mom approves of Max, then?"

"That's an understatement."

I frown at my hand then stretch my arm out straight and study it. "I've lost weight." I sit on the edge of the bed and extend my legs out before me one at a time. They're long. Obviously I haven't grown in the last year, but they're so much thinner that they look longer to me. I've taken a couple of groggy trips to the bathroom with nurses at my side, but I didn't pay much attention to my body. I certainly didn't bother to look in the mirror. Thanks to my litany of aches and pains, I was too afraid to look.

I bring my hand to my stomach and draw in a breath. This isn't my body. I've never been this thin. Not as a teenager, not as a child.

I look to Maggie. "Did this happen before or after Max started dating me?"

"After," she says carefully.

I start to stand, and she takes my arm. "I'm fine," I assure her. "I just want to look."

She ignores my protest and escorts me to the bathroom, where I freeze at the sight of myself in the mirror. These bruises on my face aren't very pretty. In fact, they almost look worse than they feel—which is saying something. But what really has me staring is the shape of my face. My cheekbones are visible, the line of my jaw more defined.

"I'll give you a minute," Maggie says. "I'll be right on the other side of the door if you need me."

After the door clicks behind her, I lift my hospital gown and study my body in the mirror. Frowning, I run my hands over my belly. It's flatter than I ever remember it being, and I can feel muscle definition beneath my stretchmark-wrinkled skin. The bruises at my ribs could get me a job starring in a domestic-violence video. Was this all really from a fall down the stairs?

I'll never have a model's body, yet I'm nearly giddy at the sight of myself. My waist is tiny for the first time in my life, my thighs toned, and the breasts I always cursed for making me look even bigger than I was are now nice curves. I'm actually excited to put on clothes and see my new body when I'm dressed like a normal person.

"It all seems too good to be true," I murmur as I study my reflection.

"Which part?" Maggie pokes her head into the bathroom just as I'm repositioning my gown. "The bruises or the traumatic brain injury?"

"You know what I mean."

She raises a brow. "You're the only person I know who could go through what you did and still think life is peachy. The rest of the world could learn a thing or two from you, Han."

I follow her out of the bathroom. "It's like a dream, you know. Suddenly, I wake up and, sure, I'm in the hospital and pretty banged up, but I have everything I've ever wanted. The business, the body—"

"You were gorgeous before," she tells me as I lower onto the edge of the bed. "You're the only one who couldn't see it."

"It's not just that."

"Max," she provides.

"Yeah." I sigh. "I feel like the universe wants me to see everything, to not take it for granted. The doctor said my memory will probably be back soon, so maybe this is the luckiest thing that's ever happened to me. How many of us get to step back from our lives and see how perfect they really are?"

"No one's life is perfect, Hanna."

"You know what I mean."

"I do know, and it worries me. You've got stars in your eyes about your life, and in a couple of days you're going to start living it again. I just don't want you to be disappointed if it isn't everything it seems."

I slouch into my pillows and take a deep breath in the silence of my hospital room.

Mom hosts brunch every Sunday at her house, and since I'm not expected to be released until tonight, she brought Sunday brunch to me this morning. My sisters were all here—Abby, Maggie, Lizzy, even Krystal, who came home from Florida when she heard about my condition. Asher stopped by. And of course, Max. Max, who hustled everyone out of the room just when I started feeling claustrophobic. Max, who managed to get my mom to change the subject when she didn't want to talk about anything but the wedding. Max, whom I caught watching me the way Asher watches Maggie, the way Will watches Cally.

A knock sounds on the door, and I expect to see Lizzy, but red curls, not blond, peek into the room.

"Are you okay?" Maggie asks. She steps in and closes the door behind her.

I swing my legs around to the floor and nod. "I'm good."

"It's all overwhelming, I bet."

"Does Mom still have him cornered?"

Maggie grins. "Yeah. I think she'd marry him herself if she could."

Toting the bag of clothes Max brought me into the bathroom, I crack the door so I can talk to Maggie. I do a double take when I see my reflection. I'll have to get used to this. I'd guess I'm at least fifty pounds lighter than I remember being. Maybe more. I knew I'd lost weight—I'd seen it for myself. Even so, when Max had first brought me clothes to wear, I couldn't believe the tiny jeans and tee in the bag would fit me. When I pull them over my hips, they slide on smooth and easy.

"She's trying to convince him to convert to Catholicism," Maggie is saying, "and Hanna, you need to tell him you don't want him to do it because I think, for you, he would."

I wash my face and brush my long hair into a high ponytail. When I return to the room, Maggie is sitting in a chair, flipping through a magazine.

Warm lips press against my neck, and I jump before realizing who's touching me. Max wraps his arms around me and pulls my back to his front. "Are you ready to get out of here?"

Leaning into his solid heat, I sigh. "More than ready."

"I have good timing, then," Nix says from the doorway.

I smile at her. After two days in the hospital and more tests than I've ever taken in my life, I've grown to like the woman. I guess this shouldn't come as a surprise, since I'm told we're friends.

"I just need to talk to Hanna about a few things and then she'll be free to go."

Maggie stands and grabs her purse. "I'll get out of the way. Call me if you need anything at all."

"I will. Thanks."

When she's gone, the doctor turns to Max. "Can I ask you to leave?"

Even though he releases me, I feel him stiffen. "She's my fiancée."

"And she'll still be your fiancée after you go down to the cafeteria for a cup of coffee." She gives him a reassuring grin. "Seriously, it's just those little HIPAA rules and my silly desire to keep my license to practice medicine."

He relaxes but seems reluctant. He brushes his thumb over my jaw and presses a soft kiss to my forehead. "I'll be back soon."

Nix follows him to the door and closes it behind him. When she comes back, she lowers herself into the chair by my bed and gives an awkward smile. "Your discharge planner met with you today and talked to you about resuming your regular activities?"

I nod. "None of that will be a problem. My whole family's on board with helping until I'm one hundred percent, and Max is just…amazing."

Nix nods. "How are you feeling about everything?"

"Other than feeling like someone decided to introduce my head to a baseball bat?" I attempt a smile.

"That's to be expected, unfortunately." She looks at her clipboard. "I wanted to talk to you about your blood work. There's nothing too alarming here, but there are some red flags with your electrolyte levels, possibly indicating malnutrition."

"Well, you're the first doctor who's ever accused me of being malnourished."

"You've lost a lot of weight the last few months, and rather quickly too. When you go home, I want you to make sure you're eating regular, balanced meals." Her brow wrinkles. "The imbalance isn't a cause for alarm at this point, but if it got worse, it could lead to kidney failure, so I want to run blood work again in a couple of weeks. I've already scheduled a follow-up appointment for you at my office." She hands me a piece of paper with a time and date.

"Thanks."

"I can only imagine what it's like to have everyone around you know more about your life than you do." She takes a deep breath. "Okay, here comes the awkward part. Are you ready?"

"Um, sure?"

She swallows and looks at her hands. "Normally, I'd call a social worker in to talk to you, but given the extenuating circumstances with your memory and our personal relationship, I wanted to do it myself. I need you to know that there are places you can call if you feel frightened or unsafe in any way. There are resources."

"Frightened of what? I don't understand."

"If there's someone in your life who's hurting you…" Nix trails off.

A chill sweeps over my skin until my bare arms are covered in goose bumps. "Who would want to hurt me?"

Nix cocks her head. "I know you don't remember your time dating Max, but I want you…" She takes another long breath and shifts awkwardly. "I'm sorry I have to ask, Hanna, but even without your memory, you know Max better than I do. Have you ever known him to be violent? Or quick to anger?"

I shake my head. "Not at all. He's just"—*the guy I always wanted*—"a really good guy."

She leans her elbows on her knees and nods. "Okay. I trust your instincts."

"What?" The implication clicks into place in my head. "You think he did this to me? You're wrong. Max is as nice as they come."

She nods again but doesn't look convinced. "Please don't be

upset. I'm not making any accusations. I want you to know you have resources. If you don't feel comfortable calling the domestic abuse hotlines, you can always call me or—"

"Nix," I say. "I promise I'll contact you personally if I don't feel completely safe." She doesn't look convinced, so I add, "I just…fell down the stairs. I've always been clumsy."

"Hanna," she says carefully, "I am suspicious that there's more to these injuries than a fall."

"What? But you said—"

"Maybe you fell down the stairs and hit your face, your ribs, your hips in the worst conceivable places. It's possible. Or maybe"— she touches her own cheekbone, pointing to the location of one of my ugliest bruises—"maybe you were beaten and then pushed."

Chapter
THREE

I'M CONFUSED when we pull up outside a building near the town square. "Where are you taking me?" God, this is awkward. Max Hallowell is driving me home. Max Hallowell is my fiancé. Max Hallowell may or may not be abusive.

No. I don't believe that. I've known Max all my life, and he's sweet. Tender. He wouldn't have pushed me down the stairs. But who? And *why*?

It's all so unbelievable that, if it weren't for these bruises, I'd think this was all some sort of elaborate practical joke.

"You live here now," he says softly. There's a little crinkle between his eyes that tells me this is all as weird for him as it is for me. "You moved here in May."

"Oh." *I* moved here. Not *we*. Is it weird that I don't live with him? Probably not. Mom still thinks it's 1950 and disapproves of "premarital cohabitation" as much as she disapproves of premarital sex. Probably more, because at least you can hide premarital sex from the neighbors. "Does Lizzy live with me?"

He shakes his head and brushes a lock of hair behind my ear. "You live here alone."

That surprises me, but I can't think about it too long because the feel of Max's rough fingers on my cheek has my eyes fluttering shut. I wonder if I've come to take this for granted. Max touching me. Max looking at me with all that tenderness in his eyes. I can't wrap my mind around the idea of this being the new normal.

"Come on." He pinches my earlobe lightly between two fingers. "I'll walk you up." He climbs out of the car and rushes around to get my door, offering his hand as I step out.

He doesn't release me when I climb onto the sidewalk, just twines his fingers through mine. The storefront before us says *Coffee, Cakes, & Confections*, and the idea of it being mine takes my breath away. I've loved the simple chemistry of cakes and cookies and scones since I was a child. The smells comfort me in a way nothing else can. Feeding other people those delicious things? The best.

He nods to the glass double doors. "That's your bakery. You have an office there to meet with clients and a kitchen in the back where you do prep, but the front is all about coffee and baked goods."

"Any good?"

"The most amazing things I've ever tasted." He presses a hand to his stomach. "I think I've gained ten pounds since you opened it."

I quirk a brow. "Can't tell."

He squeezes my hand. "Your apartment is upstairs."

We walk to the paved walkway at the back of the building, and I have to stop and smile at the gurgling water of the New Hope River. I grew up here, playing along the banks, and nothing says *home* to me like the sound and smell of the river.

I slow as we approach the stairs. They're wooden and look sturdy enough. They aren't especially steep, and it's August, so it's not like they'd be slippery with ice. Was the doctor right? Did someone push me down the stairs?

Max touches my shoulder. "Are you okay?"

"This is where it happened?"

"Lizzy found you. Thank God she came by when you didn't answer your phone."

"Does that seem as weird to you as it does to me?"

He shifts awkwardly. "I don't know, Han. My best guess is that you forgot to eat again and maybe your blood sugar tanked." He strokes my cheek with his index finger. "You've been pretty bad about that since you opened the business."

Forgetting to eat? That doesn't sound like me at all. I've *pretended* that I "forgot" to eat before, but I've never truly forgotten. Eating is my coping mechanism. My go-to when all else fails. But then again, with all the amazing things happening in my life, maybe I didn't need to cope anymore.

We take the stairs to the second floor, and I find myself hoping to feel a faulty step or find something I could have tripped over. If I'd passed out from not eating and hadn't been conscious to catch myself, would that explain the force of my fall?

When we get to the door, I rummage through my purse for my keys, but Max just grins and opens the door with a key on his ring.

He has a key to my apartment. Of course he does. We're engaged.

He flicks on the lights, illuminating a spacious, open-concept loft. To the left is a little kitchen, the right a living room, and on the back wall, against windows overlooking the New Hope River, a tiny pub-height table and four chairs.

"Wow. This is... Wow."

He cocks his head, watching me as I take in our surroundings. "Doesn't ring any bells?"

I frown. "I'm sorry. I don't remember."

He nods. We went over this again and again at the hospital. What I remember (everything before a day approximately eleven months ago) and what I don't remember (everything since), but I imagine this is as difficult for him to comprehend as it is for me.

"Well, this apartment is yours, as is the bakery."

"I still can't get over knowing I started my own business." And not just any business. A bakery. The dream.

He steps closer. "A damn good one," he whispers.

I tilt my head up to look at him. He's half a foot taller than me. I wonder if that makes it difficult to kiss while standing. I'm sure I've kissed him before. How many hundred times do you kiss a man before wearing his ring?

My heart pounds as his gaze travels from my eyes to my mouth and back. For as sweet as he's been since I woke up in the hospital, for as many times as he's kissed my hand or cheek, for as many times as he's touched me, he has yet to properly *kiss* me.

And I want to properly kiss Max more than I want to breathe.

Without the memory of his kiss, this might as well be the first time.

He skims his thumbs along either side of my jaw. "When Lizzy called and said you were at the hospital and unconscious, I was so damn worried about you. I felt like I'd lost half of myself. Don't do that to me again, okay?"

I force a laugh. "Right. I'll try not to."

His gaze dips to my mouth again. "I want to hold you and never let go, and at the same time I'm too afraid that if I let myself touch you, I'll hurt you."

"You're not going to hurt me," I whisper. *Kiss me. Please kiss me.*

Then he does. He lowers his head and sweeps his lips over mine as if it's the most natural thing in the world. As if he's done it a million times. His kiss is soft but warm, and I slide my hand into his hair to encourage him. It doesn't take much before his mouth opens over mine and I can taste his gum, his heat, his carefully harnessed control.

He's good at this, and my heart quickly goes from a nervous hammering to a stuttering, aroused racing.

He pulls me close until my breasts are pressed against his chest and I can feel the long ridge of his erection against my stomach. When he breaks the kiss and nuzzles his face into the crook of my neck, he leaves one hand at my hip, his thumb skimming the skin just above the band of my jeans.

This is my life. It doesn't seem possible.

I know he's holding back, stopping himself. By the way his fingers are curling possessively into my hip, I can tell he wants more—and I want to give him more. My heart stumbles at the idea. *More. With Max.*

Max lifts his head and runs his gaze over my face. His blue eyes have gone dark and smoky. Is that how he looks at me when I'm naked? God, I hope so. And yet, even with the changes in my body, the idea of his eyes on my nude form makes me painfully self-conscious. I've seen the women he's dated. I'll never compare to them.

"Do you need to rest or do you want me to stay for a little bit?" There's a painful edge to his voice.

"Stay." I flush and my teeth sink into my lip. "I'm a little nervous," I confess, but even as I say it, I tug his shirt from his pants and slide my hands underneath it. I've had a crush on Max since I was thirteen years old, and now I finally have permission to touch him the way I've only dreamed of before.

His stomach is washboard flat under my fingertips. As I trace the soft line of hair from his navel to the band of his jeans, his eyes float shut. His breath rushes past his parted lips. I remember admiring these abs when he was working on the deck at Arlen Fisher's cabin. I guess that would be almost a year ago now. He had sweat trickling down his chest, and he was laughing with William Bailey about something. I remember looking at him and wishing I was the kind of girl he liked. Wishing I stood a chance.

And now I'm wearing his ring.

That knowledge fills me with confidence I never imagined having, and I release the button on his jeans and slide my fingers into the band of his boxers. He hisses and staggers back half a step.

I flush with embarrassment. I shouldn't have been so bold. I shouldn't have assumed that—

"You just got out of the hospital."

One look at his face and my insecurities fall away. He's breathing hard, and there's something tortured about the way he's looking at me.

"You're not going to hurt me, Max. Please don't worry about that."

He takes my hand and leads me to the couch. He sits first, but instead of taking the seat beside him, I grasp on to this newfound confidence and straddle his hips.

He groans. "You're determined to tempt me, aren't you?"

I shift side to side, adjusting my knees until his erection puts delicious pressure between my legs.

"Hanna," he breathes.

There's something in his eyes. Something so much beyond the tenderness he showed me in the hospital. Heat. "I don't want you to hold back." I press my mouth to his, and his hands instantly find my hips, his curling fingers betraying his true desires. I want more of that, more of this evidence that this is really happening, that this is really my life.

"I can't wait to marry you," he whispers against my mouth. His fingertips roam over my jaw and across my collarbone as he shakes his head. "How did I get so lucky?"

"Tell me about our first date."

His face splits into a grin. "You want to hear about how nervous you were or where we went or—"

"How did it happen?" I settle my hand on his chest, loving the solid heat of it under my hand, the feel of his steady heartbeat. "I've had a crush on you for so long, but I thought you only had eyes for Lizzy. Did I finally work up the courage to ask you out?"

Some emotion I can't identify flashes over his face. "I asked you."

"Really?"

"You joined the gym, and I could tell you liked me." He shrugs awkwardly and slides his hands around from my hips to my ass. "Asking you to dinner was definitely the best decision I ever made in my life."

I'm engaged to Max Hallowell, and he says these amazingly sweet things to me. "Where did you take me?"

"Sebastian's."

My eyes go wide. "Fancy."

"I was determined to impress you."

"Ha! I liked you so much, you could have taken me to McDonald's and I would have been impressed."

"Hanna—"

I cut him off with my kiss. I press my lips softly to his and feel him relax underneath me. When his lips part and his hands tangle in my hair, I'm not kissing him anymore. He's kissing me. His lips are gentle and persuasive, and I'm swept into that feeling that this is all some elaborate dream. And I don't want to wake up.

By the time our lips part, we're both breathing heavily, and

I lean my forehead against his. "What are we going to do if my memory doesn't come back?" I whisper. The question has been nagging at me. "We're supposed to be getting married and I've lost the entirety of our relationship. This must be so terrible for you."

His eyes go wide. "You're worried about *me*?"

"It doesn't seem fair to ask you to start over."

"I'm not marrying your memories. I'm marrying you. And I would start over happily for you."

"This is all so surreal. I just keep waiting to wake up and find out it was all a dream."

He untangles his hands from my hair and slips them under my shirt. His touch is light and cautious of my bruises, but when his fingertips skim the underside of my breasts, he's confident and sure—a wanderer returning to familiar territory. His thumbs find my nipples and my breath draws in with a hiss. I collapse forward, resting my head on his shoulder.

"I'm here," he whispers in my ear as his fingers work delicious magic under my shirt. "And I'm real."

I roll my hips against his erection, and I can't deny it. He's real. And he's amazing.

I slide my hand between our bodies and find his hard-on.

"We shouldn't do this," he groans. His lips sample the side of my neck between his words. "Not until you're better. Not until we've really had a chance to talk."

I know this isn't the first time we've touched. It couldn't possibly be. If I wanted to release him from his jeans and take him into my mouth, it surely wouldn't be the first time for that either.

In the war between my desires and my self-conscious nerves, my nerves are winning, and I won't have that. If this is my new amazing life, I'm going to live it up.

"I guess it's stupid that I'm so nervous," I whisper.

"It isn't. Not at all."

Anything else he planned to say is cut off by his groan as I unzip his jeans and release him from his boxers with one bold move of my hand.

My breath catches at the sight of him, long and thick and hard. For me. I lick my lips, wrap my hand around his shaft, and stroke.

"Jesus." His eyes float closed and his hips buck instinctively, moving him hard against the grip of my hand.

My nerves flitter away as he gets lost in my touch. He fights to keep his eyes open, his control intact. I may be a little on the inexperienced side, but I know how to give a damn good hand job. I had one asshole boyfriend my freshman year in college who demanded them regularly. Once, I regretted that relationship, but suddenly it feels worth it because I love the pleasure on Max's face— the way he looks at me through his lashes, the way his nostrils flare as I use my thumb to test the moisture at the tip of his cock.

"Hanna," he chokes out, and I squeeze him a little harder. I can tell he's close by the way he's swelling. Harder. Thicker.

I push off him and to my knees on the floor, never releasing him.

He reaches for me, but I ignore his hands and lick the swollen head of his dick.

"Oh, fuck."

I grin because he's lost the battle with his self-control I never intended to let him win.

I release him just long enough to slide my tongue up the underside of his shaft, and his body shudders. When I stretch my lips over him and take him deep, he groans, and I feel beautiful and powerful. My body winds tight with arousal.

Max puts a gentle hand on my face. "You don't have to—"

I pull him deeper before he can say anything else. I don't remember doing this before—blowjobs are definitely not in the limited realm of my remembered experience—but sixty seconds in, I can already tell what feels good to him and what makes him nearly lose control.

I work my tongue over the underside of him and add more suction to my movement. His gentle hand moves to my head and slides into my hair. He leads me to take him half an inch deeper. Before I can even adjust to the new depth, he's coming, filling my throat in a way I never would have imagined could be so sexy.

Yet a smile curves my lips as I release him, as happy as I am turned on. And *fuck* am I turned on.

He pulls me into his lap and gathers me against him.

"That was amazing," I murmur into his chest.

His body shakes with his nearly silent chuckle. "I'm pretty sure that's my line."

"I know you were trying not to go there tonight, but..." I sigh and grin up at him. "I couldn't help myself."

He kisses me firmly, tongue sweeping into my mouth, teeth nipping my lips. Then his hand is under my shirt again, doing delicious things to my nipples, and I hope he never stops.

"I like that so much," I breathe into his ear, and he moans and rolls a nipple between two fingers. He slides his other hand between my legs. I come up on my knees to get a better angle. As I rock into his hand, a desperate moan slips from my lips, and he gives me the extra pressure I need. My body might be beaten and tender, but I've had years of fantasies about this man. I don't have the patience to wait now that I have him at my fingertips.

More pressure between my legs. The hem of my jeans presses into my swollen clit, and I grind harder, but I need more. I need slick skin and rough fingers and—

"Ack!"

The sound of a woman's screech has me jumping off the couch. My feet tangle under me and I go down, falling to the floor and knocking my head on the glass coffee table.

Max's eyes go to the door, where my mom's standing, her back already turned to us, her hand thrown over her eyes.

"Shit," he mutters.

"I didn't see anything," Mom sing-songs. "Just here to check on my daughter and drop off some groceries." She hoists a plastic bag into the air as evidence.

Max quickly pulls himself together, zipping his pants before sinking to the floor next to me. "Are you okay?"

I rub my head where it hit the table. "I'm fine." A little mortified that my mother just walked in on me grinding myself against Max's hand. But hey, I'm an optimist, and the optimist in me is just glad she didn't find her way in the front door, say, five minutes earlier— when I was on my knees.

"We didn't lock the door, did we?" he whispers.

"Apparently not."

"Yeah, next time—"

"Absolutely."

He helps me off the floor, and I give my girlie parts a silent little lecture about patience because they're down there whimpering, *"Not fair! Make her leave! Things were just getting good!"*

"Is everyone decent?" Mom asks, already turning around.

"Now we are," I say under my breath. "Mom, maybe you should knock next time?"

"You just got out of the hospital. I didn't think..." In her defense, her cheeks are beet red, and I'm fairly confident she will be knocking next time. And every time after. "I was young once too. I remember those weeks leading up to my wedding. Your father and I could hardly—"

"Mom. Please?" Somehow I don't think hearing about how horny she was before marrying Dad is actually going to make this situation less awkward.

"I'm just here to make sure you don't need anything, but obviously Max was taking care of you—"

"Mom!"

She throws her hand over her mouth, but I can see her smile peeking out the sides. "I didn't mean it like that." She drops her hand and sighs as she sets the single bag of groceries on the counter.

"Thanks for checking on her and"—Max rubs the back of his neck—"sorry about that."

She waves away his apology. "So we haven't had a chance to really celebrate your engagement, what with this accident nonsense. Max, would you allow me to host an engagement party at my house? I don't want to be the over-intruding mother-in-law, but I would really love to celebrate."

Max wraps his arms around me from behind and kisses my hair. I love that he seems to always be touching me. Like he can't help himself. "That would be wonderful, Mrs. Thompson. There's nothing I want to celebrate as much as Hanna agreeing to marry me."

She presses her hand to her chest and tears swell in her eyes. "It does my heart good to see you two together and so happy. The news of your engagement was what really got me through worrying about my daughter."

"I'm okay, Mom."

She nods and blinks away her tears. "I know, I know. But it was a shock. Oh, look at me! Keeping you up when you should be getting your rest."

Even after her touching display of emotion, I want her to leave so I can be alone with Max again. I blame those girlie parts down south. They apparently have a mind of their own, and an active imagination to go with it.

Mom adjusts her purse on her shoulder. "Try to sleep tonight. I know it's hard, but it's important if you're going to recover."

"I will," I promise.

Mom turns her smile on my fiancé. "Max, would you be a doll and walk me out? I know you need to get going too."

Max nods, and it takes everything in me to keep the smile on my face. *Effing seriously? He's leaving me?*

"Of course I will." He winks at me. "You know how to get me if you need me."

If I need him? I would have thought that was obvious.

Chapter
FOUR

ALMOST PERFECT.

I'm surveying my life as if from the outside, and that's how it looks to me. Almost perfect. Sure, I have these bruises and I'm banged up from my fall, but everything else? My apartment. My business. My body. *Max...*

He looks at me like I'm the most precious thing in the world. And I'm wearing his ring. I might not remember how my life got like this, but I'll do whatever it takes to keep it this way.

I wander around my apartment, feeling a bit like a rude visitor peeping in on someone else's life. The kitchen is clean, the refrigerator full of water bottles, apples, and carrot sticks. The freezer isn't much better, with little more than frozen berries and chicken breasts, and the pantry is sparse. Mom brought me a half-gallon of milk and some fresh fruit, but I still need to go grocery shopping. I find a notepad on the counter and start a list:

Grocery shopping: Bread, milk, cereal, pasta

I stop writing and stare at the list I've made. These were foods I ate before. What do I eat now? I'll have to be careful about what I buy. I'm sure I worked hard to lose this weight.

My mind goes to the stairs again. The fall. Max's words about low blood sugar and me forgetting to eat. Was that really all there was to it, or did I have to live on the meager basics in my kitchen to get this thin?

I shake away the thought. If I'd developed unhealthy habits, my sisters would have put a stop to it. Anyway, however I got here, I don't want to ruin my progress. Especially if we're planning a wedding.

A thrill runs through me at the thought. A wedding. I'm marrying Max.

But as I go to return the notepad to the basket, a small slip of paper falls out.

It's a prescription for an antidepressant. And it's dated one week ago. Why would I need that?

My phone buzzes on the counter, and I tuck the script into the bottom of the basket for safekeeping before grabbing my cell. I don't recognize the number on the display, and I'm not in the mood to chat anyway, so I send the call to voicemail.

As I wander the living room area, I spot a laptop on the desk in the corner. I immediately open it, ready to peek into the last year of my life the way a stranger might—social media. A dialogue box pops up on the screen and asks for my password. I tap in my birthday, but it doesn't take. I try my initials and my birthday. Still nothing. Those have always been my go-to passwords. I'll have to ask Max if he knows what it is. Maybe I used our first date or his pet name for me.

The bedroom is tidy, save for a basket of unfolded laundry in one corner. The closet isn't overly full, but I have a nice collection of jeans and shirts in my new smaller size and a slew of black workout capris and tank tops.

It's a small apartment so it doesn't take me long to see everything. I should take a shower and try to get some sleep. Tomorrow I want to learn all I can about my business and see what I need to do to catch up from my hospital stay. The idea of the water hitting my bruises with any pressure at all is more than I can bear, so I run a bath instead and sigh as I sink into the warm water. I release my hair from its clip and let it fall down my back.

When it's just me and the lulling beat of the water pouring into the tub, I let myself think about Max and what we might be doing if my mother hadn't come over tonight.

I skim my fingertips over my breasts and imagine him stripping off my shirt and releasing my heavy breasts from my bra. I squeeze my nipples with the thought of Max taking them into his mouth. Men have always liked my breasts, and I love having them played with, squeezed, sucked. Would he have kept me in his lap, his hand stroking me through my jeans as he sucked and played? Or would he have taken me to my bedroom so he could lay me down and explore my body?

My mind latches on to that image—a bare-chested Max hovering over me in bed, unzipping my jeans and dragging them down my hips as he sucked my nipple into his mouth, laved it with his tongue.

These aren't new fantasies, but knowing Max is mine now heightens their intensity. This "what if" could just as well be our "next time." Remembering how good it felt to have his hand between my legs and his breath in my hair, I'm already close when I slip my hand into the hot water and find my swollen flesh. I'm so wrapped in the fantasy that the hand isn't mine anymore. It's Max's. His hot mouth is open against my neck, and all he has to do is slip a finger inside me—*God, yes, like that.* I imagine his hand, his hot breath at my ear, his groan. I cling to the thought and I come.

After I wash my hair, dry off, and put on my pajamas, I lock the door and pad to bed with my phone in my hand. When I climb in, I pull up the text messages on my phone and enter Max's name.

Hanna: I hate that you had to leave when you did.
Max: You and me both. Are you okay?
Hanna: I am now. Took a bath and imagined how things could have gone if my mom hadn't shown up.
Max: Want to tell me about it?
Hanna: The bath? It was what you'd expect. Hot. Wet.
Max: You're killing me.
Hanna: That'll teach you to choose walking my mom to her car over finishing things with me.
Max: Lesson learned.

I wake up to someone climbing into bed next to me, hot, hard muscle cozying up behind me.

I blink away sleep. Max is in my bed and I want to enjoy it, enjoy him, but sleep has such a tight hold on me I can hardly keep my eyes open. I snuggle as close to him as I can get, but sleep is already tugging me back down.

"Couldn't stay away?" I murmur in the darkness.

"You know I can't," he whispers against my ear. His voice is different somehow. Deeper? Maybe sleepy? I don't have time to think about it because I'm wrapped up in his heat, his bare chest against my back, one of his hands right between my breasts, and I can't fight it when my dreams suck me back in. But somehow, with his heat against me and his arms around me, my fitful dreams fade away and I don't just sleep. I rest.

When I wake again, the room is still dark, but Max's mouth is doing delicious things to the side of my neck. I arch against him and am greeted by the hard length of his erection against my ass. I have to bite my lip at the thrill that rushes through me. Not only can I do that to him, but he wanted me enough that he had to come back tonight.

Under my shirt, his fingertips skim the underside of my breasts, and a soft moan slips from my lips. He cups my breast in his hot hand and grazes his callused palm against my nipple, toys and teases until it's hard and tight under his hand and I am rocking back into him instinctively.

"Jesus, I missed you so much." His voice sounds funny, but I hardly have time for the thought to register before he's squeezing my nipples, sending electric jolts of pleasure from my breasts and right up through my center. His touch is harder than it was earlier. Rougher. But I like it. He's so good at this. He knows exactly how to touch me, exactly how much pressure I like. I wouldn't want him to ever stop touching my breasts if it weren't for this nearly painful ache that's been pulsing between my legs since we were interrupted in my living room—the ache my own touch couldn't quite ease.

I circle my hips and rub my backside against his erection. Thick and wild arousal buzzes through me, electric and sharp with its intensity. He wants me as much as I want him.

"Touch me," I whisper into the darkness. "I need you to touch me."

He groans against my neck and then his fingers are dipping into the waistband of my sleep pants.

I turn in his arms just as his hand meets the hot and needy place between my thighs. Our mouths touch in the darkness, and something niggles at the back of my mind. Something's changed between last night and now. Does he smell different or—

The thought disintegrates as he slides a finger inside me. I can't believe how slick and wet I am. Except that this is Max and I need his touch.

I rock against him, letting him touch me the way I touched myself in the bath. Only this is hotter. Sweeter. More intense. Not just because it's him. It's almost as if he knows what I like better than I do. His finger moves inside me and his teeth nip at my neck almost painfully. But I like it. I want more of this unbridled lust, more of his expert touch.

He withdraws his finger and replaces it with two, stretching me in a way that has my body pulsing around him in response.

"Yes," I whisper. I want this. Need it.

His thumb finds my clit and his fingers curl.

"Oh God…" Am I a screamer? I bite my lip, but holy shit, I can't—

"Let me hear you scream," he growls in my ear, his stubble scraping at the tender skin of my neck. "Let me feel you pulse around my fingers as you come."

I curl my nails into his forearm, not to stop him, but because this pleasure inside me is so intense I have to do something, put this energy somewhere.

His other hand slides up my side and squeezes right at the bruise on my ribs. Pain vibrates through me, and I cry out.

"Hanna?" He pulls away and clicks on the light.

I'm still wincing at the pain from my manhandled bruise when

I look at him through squinted eyes.

And then I scream.

I shove the man off me as hard as I can. My mind gropes for the lessons I learned in the personal defense class I took in college. I bring up my knee, aiming for his balls.

He lets out an airy *oomph,* and I flail, backing as far away from him as I can get. I fall off the bed, and the impact of my already-battered body slamming into the floor has me crying out.

"Jesus, Hanna!" the man—who is definitely not Max—says from the bed. "What the fuck was that for?"

Oh God. He knows my name.

I'm trembling.

My phone is on the bedside table, and I scramble to get to it before he can take it away.

"I'll call the police!" I warn, holding the phone up like it's a weapon.

The man on the bed is white-faced and stricken and looking at me like I've lost my mind.

"You can't just come into a woman's house and get into her bed." Shit. Now I'm trying to reason with a sex offender. Jesus. But he's just sitting there. Is that *normal*?

His expression goes from confused to desolate as he skims his eyes over my bruised face. "Damn. What happened to you, angel?"

I fumble with my phone, pressing the button on the side and trying to get it to light up. Nothing. It's dead. Why didn't I charge it before I fell asleep last night?

He pushes off the bed, and I back into a corner, arms wrapped around myself. "Leave. Please."

He holds up his hands and takes a step toward me. "Hanna, baby. Tell me what happened. Tell me—"

I press my body as close to the wall as I can. I should have locked myself in the bathroom or something. I am one of those too-dumb-to-live heroines you see in horror movies. Especially since the thing keeping me here—keeping me from running to *safety*—is the hurt on his face. I've always been the kind of person who tries to make people happy, but this is ridiculous.

Think, Hanna. Okay, I'll need a description for the cops. Tall—

taller than Max, maybe—messy dark hair, an Incredible Hulk tattoo on his right shoulder, some numbers tattooed above his left pec. God, is he an ex-con? Don't convicts get numbers tattooed on themselves?

He steps closer, and a shudder runs through me.

"Please don't hurt me." I sink to the floor and cross my arms in front of my face.

His gaze catches on my left hand, and his jaw goes hard. "I see." He backs off and grabs something off the floor. Then he's tugging a shirt over his head. It falls into place and covers that amazing body.

Amazing body? What the eff is wrong with me?

As stupid as it is, I don't believe this man is here to hurt me. There's nothing intimidating about his body language, and even though his face has gone hard and angry, there's no violence in his eyes.

He grabs his jeans. "You could have told me."

"I don't know what you're talking about." My voice cracks.

Jeans unbuttoned and half up his hips, he's heading toward the door. Stupidly, I follow him. My hands are shaking, my head spinning.

He grabs the doorknob and goes still, but he doesn't look at me. "When I was touching you just now"—he swallows—"you thought I was…"

"I thought you were my fiancé." The whisper seems to swell in the small space and vibrate off the walls.

He punches the wall beside the door. "You and Max have a nice life." Then he's leaving, slamming the door behind him and making the whole room rattle. And me right along with it.

Chapter
FIVE

"So did Max stay over last night?" Lizzy sets a steaming mug of black coffee in front of me and stirs cream into her own, all the while avoiding my gaze.

"Can I have some of that?"

"Cream? As in, empty calories? For healthier-than-thou Hanna?"

I've been drinking coffee since I was sixteen, and I've been taking cream in it for just as long. I try a sip without and shake my head. My memory loss apparently includes how to enjoy black coffee. "Yes, please." I snag the cream before she can make any more comments.

We're at a table in the front of my bakery, the OPEN sign glowing into the darkness of Main Street.

I convinced myself not to call her last night. I'd wanted to. I'd been confused and scared, and the most natural instinct had been to call Liz. After the man left my apartment, I ran to find my phone charger and plug in my phone. I stared at the screen as it came to life, but I kept thinking of the way the man's face had changed when his gaze landed on my ring. My mind kept repeating the deep rumble of his voice as he'd said, *"You and Max have a nice life."*

It wasn't confusion or fear that made me decide not to call her. As I sank to the edge of my bed and settled my head in my hands, adrenaline still hummed through my veins, but the frantic, clawing fear was gone. In its place boiled red-hot *shame*.

"So, Max?" Lizzy asks. She holds up her hands. "Not that it's my business."

There's something different in our relationship. We could always say anything to each other, though we often didn't have to. An exchanged glance was usually enough to let her know how I was feeling. But there's a rift between us now. I can sense it even if I can't explain it. I noticed first at the hospital—not so much by the way she acted when she was around, but more because of how often she *wasn't* around. I kept expecting her to be the one coming into my room to keep me company, but nine times out of ten, it was someone else.

All my life, people have asked me what it's like to be a twin. They want me to explain our connection. Trying to explain to someone what it's like to have a twin sister is like trying to explain what it's like to have a pulse. I don't know any other way. All I know is that her smile is attached to my heart. I float when she's happy, and when she's sad, my world is a puzzle with a missing piece.

But right now that connection is gone. I want to blame the amnesia, but I'm pretty sure that's just the optimism thinking.

"Max didn't stay," I say cautiously.

She rolls her eyes and mutters something I can't quite make out. "*Goody two-shoes,*" maybe? She wouldn't call me that if she knew I woke up to another man in my bed. "Any progress with your memory?"

I shake my head. "Not yet. Patience, right?" Patience. I'm engaged to marry the man of my dreams, who I might or might not have been cheating on. Waiting for my memories to return should be a piece of cake.

"Well, patience isn't going to run this bakery," Liz mutters. "In the meantime, I'd better bring you up to speed."

She gives me a tour of my bakery. The front area is small but serviceable. It has four tables and a bar along the wall with outlets. "So people who are working on their laptops don't hog the tables,"

Lizzy explains. The glass cases in the front feature everything from freshly baked Italian bread and croissants to cupcakes and fresh pastries.

"My mouth is watering just looking at all of it."

Lizzy snorts. "You don't touch it. Not a grain of sugar has passed those lips in at least three months."

"Nothing tastes as good as thin feels, I guess?"

"Clearly the amnesia has wiped away all memory of your cheese Danish. Maggie declared it foodgasmic, and she's not wrong. And your chocolate croissants?" She closes her eyes and bites her lower lip.

"You're making me hungry," I complain.

Her lips quirk into a lopsided smile. "Good. I didn't think you were capable of hunger anymore. Maybe the amnesia fixed you." She leads the way past the glass cases and through the doors to the gleaming stainless-steel kitchen at the back. Ovens line one wall, and another has a row of walk-in coolers.

"Holy crap," I breathe. "How did I afford this place?"

"You didn't. You had some silent partner backing you, so money wasn't an issue."

"Silent partner? Who?"

She shrugs. "I don't know. You were all mysterious about it. We thought it might have been Asher, but when Maggie asked him, he said he didn't have anything to do with it. Mom thinks maybe it was Max, but that doesn't explain why you'd be secretive about it. But *somebody* came in here and renovated the building and got you your little start-up."

"It's probably in my paperwork, huh?"

She shrugs. "I guess."

"I'm just surprised Mom didn't try to talk me out of it. You know how she's felt most of her life about my baking."

"She wasn't thrilled about your choice, but you could pretty much do no wrong in her eyes since you started dating Max." There's something snide about the way she says it, as if I dated Max and improved my relationship with my mom all to irritate her.

"I can't believe I took the plunge. That doesn't seem like me."

"You haven't seemed much like yourself for a while now," she says, but I don't think the words are for me. She shakes her head and waves away the subject. "You had a wedding last weekend while you were in the hospital. You'd already gotten the cake finished, so Maggie and I handled it for you, but you probably want to call the bride when she gets back from her honeymoon next week."

The bride. Because I make wedding cakes.

"I've been taking care of the bread orders for the restaurants and grocers who contract with you. Drew has been keeping up with the baking for the front, but school's going to start soon. She won't be able to put in the hours she has been."

"Drew?"

"Cally's sister."

I shake my head. "I know who she is. I guess I'm just surprised she works for me."

"She started the week you opened. She's a good little worker as long as you can keep her off her phone and away from the customers. Customer service isn't her forte."

I grin at the image of Cally's know-it-all teenage sister struggling to be kind to sorority girls ordering non-fat, sugar-free, extra-hot, double-shot mochas.

"You have a wedding this weekend, so we'll need to find time to get the cake made and decorated. I can try to help if you don't remember, but honestly, the decorating part has always been your baby and I pretty much suck at it."

"Wait. So you work with me?"

She lifts a brow. "I'm pretty sure you think of it as me working *for* you, but yes. I haven't gotten a teaching job, and I work for my sister like a loser."

"You work *with* me, and I think that's awesome."

She rolls her eyes. "Anyway, you have three meetings with upcoming brides this week."

"Wow." I turn a slow circle. "I can't believe how quickly it's taken off."

My stomach twists as I scan the gleaming stainless-steel countertops. I've been so hung up on my new body and my engagement to Max, I haven't had the chance to think much about this part of my life. How am I supposed to run my business if I don't even remember what recipes I use or what clients I've promised cakes to?

"I don't even know where I buy supplies," I mutter to myself.

Lizzy's cool fingers gently squeeze my forearm. "It's going to be okay." Her eyes connect with mine, and for a split second, it's back—that connection between us flickers like lights in a storm. "You should come to Maggie and Asher's with me tonight. Asher and Nate are having a jam session and they're making a get-together out of it."

"Nate who?"

"Crap. I guess you probably don't even remember him. Nate Crane? You know, sexy rocker?" She frowns. "I guess you wouldn't know. He was kind of an unknown before, but he's been touring with Asher, and his single is really shooting up the charts."

"Cool." I shift. Partying it up at Asher's doesn't appeal to me right now. After my middle-of-the-night visitor, I just want to spend my evening with Max and reassure myself that everything is okay. "I'll probably take a rain check, though."

"Oh." She sounds disappointed. Really disappointed. Like she was counting on me. "Okay, well, that's fine."

And just like that, the flickering light of our connection is snuffed out again.

"What happened to us?"

"What?"

"You and me. Why are you mad at me?"

"I don't know what you're talking about."

"Come on, Liz. This is us. Something's not right."

Lizzy shifts her gaze away. "Truth be told, you and I haven't exactly been close lately."

"Why?"

She shrugs. "I don't know. You started dating Max, and it was okay at first, but then you were running all the time and you were losing weight and—"

"You stopped being close to me because I lost weight?"

"Jesus! No. Of course not. You're the one who pulled away." She cuts her eyes to the floor and bites her lip. "At least that's how it felt to me, but I might have been uncomfortable with all the changes you were making. It just didn't seem healthy, ya know?"

"Getting healthy didn't seem healthy?"

She throws up her hands. "See? You're so defensive about it! We could never talk, and when we did, all you cared about was Max and running, and I didn't even recognize you anymore."

My eyes fill with tears. "I thought you of all people would be happy for me when I finally got some goodness in my life."

"Is it good, Hanna? Are you so sure?" She stares at me for a long time, that little wrinkle appearing between her blond brows.

The bell over the front door rings, ending our staring contest.

When we go out front, we find Mom and Granny behind the front counter, preparing themselves cups of coffee, Mom a flurry of anxious gestures in her pink business suit and Granny serene in her wrinkled cotton hippie skirt.

"Your first day out of the hospital and you're already back at work," Mom lectures.

"I'm fine," I assure her.

"You're not fine. You've had a bad fall and you need to recover."

"The doctor said I could get back to my normal routine. She said it might even be good for me."

Mom grins. "And you know what else will be good for you?"

"I can guess," Lizzy grumbles.

"I have appointments scheduled with three different possible wedding venues," Mom says. "I thought, what better way to recuperate than to focus on something that makes you happy? Something good."

"I don't know if I can—"

"I won't hear any objections. You're my daughter, and I'm going to make sure you take care of yourself these next few weeks." She tilts my chin up and moves my face side to side, inspecting my bruises. If she thinks those are bad, she should see what's going on under my shirt. "I bet you'll be healed enough for a wedding in as soon as a month."

Lizzy chokes on her coffee, and I gape at my mother. "A month?"

Granny tsks. "Don't rush the girl, Gretchen."

"Why you would drag your feet when a man like Max wants to

marry you is beyond me."

"I'm not dragging my feet," I object, but I kind of am. Because don't I need answers before I can say my vows to Max? Don't I need my memories?

"So it's settled. We'll spend tomorrow looking at wedding venues."

"I can't just set a date without talking to Max," I object.

Mom waves away my concern. "It's the wedding. All men worry about is the bachelor party and the wedding night. Besides, we need to know what dates the venue you want is available. *Then* we'll talk about setting a date."

I try to take deep breaths, but I keep thinking about the man in my apartment, about all the things I *don't* know about the last year. My headache is back and nausea rolls over me. I brace myself on the counter.

"See, Gretchen?" Granny scolds. "You're stressing her out."

"I'm okay," I lie. "I'm just a little overwhelmed. I need Lizzy to bring me up to date on work stuff and I'll feel better."

Mom rolls her eyes then sighs. "Fine. I'll pick you up tomorrow at noon. Elizabeth, don't you dare let your sister do any work."

"Yes, ma'am," Lizzy says, irritation clear in her voice.

The women take their coffee and push through the door. A hot billow of August air fills the store as the door floats closed.

"Come on," Lizzy says. "Let's get some baking done before you have to spend all your waking hours planning your happily-ever-after."

My phone buzzes from the pocket of my apron. I wipe my hands on a towel and pull it out.

Appointment with Doc Perkins.

I frown at the calendar reminder. Do I know a Dr. Perkins?

I move to the sink and turn the water on with the back of my hand. Once it's hot, I wash my hands with soap and water, dry them, and grab my phone again.

I have no idea how I managed to lose so much weight while doing this job. A single morning in my bakery and I'm jacked up on dozens of taste tests. A little bite of this treat, a sample of that frosting. I practically have a stomach ache. Thank God for my compulsive organization. It was relatively easy to find all my recipes. I was preparing gum-paste calla lilies for this weekend's wedding cake when my phone buzzed, but I can finish up later.

The reminder doesn't have a phone number or an address, so I pull up the browser on my phone and do a quick search. "Dr. Perkins New Hope" doesn't get me any hits, so I try "Dr. Perkins Indianapolis."

Dr. Perkins, MD, Psychiatry

A psychiatrist?

I scroll through my calendar, moving back through the past three months, but I only see one appointment with the doctor listed and it was a week ago. Was I going to start regular appointments? Why? For pointers on keeping brides calm? Or maybe the doctor is the silent partner Liz told me about?

Right. The relationship is a business one and you just happen to have a script for antidepressant in your apartment.

This doctor must have some answers to the endless questions that have taken up residence in my brain. I highlight the address in my browser and send it to my phone's navigation system.

I've already grabbed my keys when I pause. I'm not supposed to drive. But I'm not sure I want anyone to know I'm seeing a psychiatrist, and how can I have someone drive me without spilling the beans?

"Liz," I call to the front, pocketing my keys, "I need to leave for a few hours."

I wait for her to ask where I'm going, but she just shrugs. Her disinterest is another reminder of the distance between us. I'm not used to this, but I don't have time to think about it much. I'm too busy planning to break doctor's orders and drive to Indianapolis.

By the time I get to Dr. Perkins's office, I'm fifteen minutes late to my appointment. The receptionist's eyes go big when he sees my face. "What happened to you?"

"I got in a fight with a flight of stairs. I lost."

"Yikes." He stands and ushers me through a heavy walnut door.

On the other side, a woman is sitting behind a desk, tapping at her computer. Her face lights up then shrinks in rapid succession when she sees me. "Hanna! What happened?"

"I'll leave you," the receptionist says.

As the heavy door closes, the doctor motions to an overstuffed chair and steeples her fingers as I sit. "Tell me what's going on, Hanna."

"You're Dr. Perkins?"

Her tiny face draws into a tight frown. "Of course I am."

"And I'm…one of your patients?"

Her frown turns to skepticism.

"I took a fall." I motion to my face. I explain as briefly as I can about my amnesia, telling her I'm here because of the reminder on my phone.

"Oh, dear. I wish I would have known. I would have come to the hospital and consulted with your doctor."

I'm glad she didn't. I don't think I want my friends and family to know I've sought out therapy. "I don't understand." I don't want to offend this woman. She seems very nice. "It shows in my calendar that I've been here before, and I found a prescription for antidepressants in my apartment, but…" I'm not sure how to say it.

"Go on," she prods.

"My life seems perfect. I have my own business that seems to be going great, and I'm engaged to marry an amazing man. I feel okay about my body for the first time in my life. Why would I need to see a psychiatrist? Why would I need antidepressants?" *Why would I cheat on my loving fiancé?*

She folds her arms and studies me, her face a series of hard and soft lines I can neither read nor recognize. "Do you think only people who have something 'wrong' with their lives need to seek help for their mental health?"

"Of course not. I just—" I cut myself off at her raised eyebrows. Apparently she's a no-nonsense woman. "I wouldn't put it that way. I thought that if I was seeing you and you'd prescribed antidepressants, there had to be a reason."

She's silent for a long moment that catapults me back in time to just after my father's death. I was a teenager, and Daddy was my world. Back then, I never measured up with Mom. She was always trying to fix me—shrink me, tone me, dress me, make me an acceptable representation of her family. Something she wouldn't find so shameful. But Daddy was happy to let me be. Then he died, and after the funeral, the school therapist called us down one at a time. "Why do you think you're here?" he asked me, his voice sounding more bored than empathetic, and he let the silence grow bigger and stranger between us until I answered.

But I'm not that girl anymore. I'm not the fat teenager languishing in her gorgeous sisters' shadows. I'm not the ignored child striving for perfection in all things to make up for her appearance.

Sure, I'm overweight, but look at my grades!

Sure, I can't fit into the pants in your average store, but I'm always happy.

Sure, I can't get a date to save my life, but I'm the best friend a girl could ever have.

I'm exhausted just thinking about it.

But she isn't like the school counselor and she doesn't let the silence go on forever. "You came to me because you were battling depression and an eating disorder."

I feel myself wilt. I don't want to hear these things. I don't want her tainting my perfect world. I shouldn't have come. I should have ignored the reminder and carried on.

"Tell me what you're thinking," Dr. Perkins says.

I remember Nix's request for me to see her in her office about diet concerns brought on by my blood work. "An eating disorder? Depression?"

Something flicks across her features. Regret? Sadness? "There's no shame in getting help. Are you eating? Since your accident?"

I pause and turn back to her. "I am."

She smiles. "That's good."

"I wasn't before, was I? That's how I lost all this weight? I was starving myself?" Panic claws at me the moment the words leave my mouth because I know they're true. "This means I'm going to gain the weight back, doesn't it?"

"You came to me because you recognized something in your own habits that you knew wasn't healthy. You recognized there were parts of your life more important than numbers on the scale and you wanted me to help."

I swallow, but this information is a bitter pill that goes down rough and painfully. "Did I talk to you about…other things?"

"Like what?"

"This is confidential?" I whisper.

"Of course."

"Was I cheating on my fiancé?" I shake my head. "He's my fiancé now, but I guess he would have been my boyfriend last time I was here."

She crosses her arms over her chest. "You didn't share that with me if it was true, but you didn't mention a boyfriend either."

"Oh. Yeah. I guess this was just about the food."

"Eating disorders are *never* just about the food, Hanna. They're about more than your body and about more than losing weight. They're about control. And you've spent the last three months starving yourself so you would feel like you had control over your life again."

Chapter
SIX

WHEN I return from Indianapolis, the bakery is bustling with a crowd picking up lattes for their afternoon pick-me-ups and fresh pastries to go along with them.

Squeezing past the line, I slip behind the counter and tap Lizzy's shoulder. "I need to talk."

"Yeah, well, I'm a little busy running your bakery, so—"

I take the cup from her hand and slam it on the counter. "It's important."

"PMS much?" the ponytailed pretty girl at the front of the line says.

I narrow my eyes at her before sticking my head back in the kitchen. "Drew? I need you to work the front for a few minutes."

"That's a really bad idea," Lizzy warns.

I ignore her and drag her up to my apartment. It's tempting to meet her chilliness with my own, but right now I need my sister too much. I slam the door closed behind her.

"Listen." I wag my finger in her face. I've had enough. "I don't know who pissed in your Wheaties, but right now I need my sister, so whatever is broken between us, can we just put it aside for a while?"

Her eyes go wide. "I... You..." Her shoulders sag and she

collapses onto my couch.

"You asked me if I was sure things are good. Well, I'm not sure." I pace in front of her. "Everything looks so perfect on the surface, but how am I supposed to know how I feel about anything when I don't remember?"

"I'm such a bitch, Hanna. I'm sorry. Don't listen to me. I'm jealous. You're engaged, Maggie's living with Asher... Any minute now, I'm going to be the last single girl standing. Maybe that's making me cranky, but it shouldn't ruin a happy time for you."

"I think maybe I'm cheating on Max," I blurt.

"Shit, Han-Han. What happened?"

I sink onto the couch next to her and lean my head on her shoulder. She combs my hair with her fingers, and even though the contact feels awkward and unsure, it relaxes me.

"It's going to be okay," she murmurs in my ear.

She doesn't rush me, and I let myself take my time because suddenly it's all too much—the last few days, the injuries, the amnesia, the engagement, the whole new life. As much as I'd like Max to be able to comfort me, he's still a stranger to me in a lot of ways. But Lizzy's part of me. We sit, letting the minutes pass and the silence slowly stitch us back together.

I don't know how much time has passed when I finally sit up and wipe my eyes.

"Coffee?" she asks.

I nod and follow her to the kitchen, where I sit on a stool as she prepares us a fresh pot. "While Max and I were dating, do you know if I was...seeing anyone else?"

She turns to cock a brow at me. "Seeing anyone else? Miss Goody Two-Shoes date two guys at once? *As if.*"

Right. It doesn't sound like me. But how does that explain what happened last night? *Better come out with it, girl.* "Max didn't stay over last night, but I didn't sleep alone either."

Her jaw goes slack and those gorgeous baby blues of hers widen. "What? Who? Why? Does Max know?"

"All very good questions."

She prepares my coffee and hands me my mug. I wrap my hands around it, letting it warm my hands instead of drinking it.

"Are you going to tell me who else you're sleeping with," Lizzy huffs, "or are you going to make me guess?"

"Someone slid into my bed last night. I was sleeping and assumed it was Max, but then we started fooling around in the middle of the night, and when he turned on the light, I realized it...wasn't."

"Someone slipped into bed with you while you were sleeping, and it *wasn't* Max?"

I watch her carefully. "No."

"Holy shit. Who was it?"

"I have no idea. He was a stranger to me."

She slams her mug down and coffee sloshes onto the counter. "Why aren't we calling the cops?"

"Because I don't think we need to."

"You're freaking kidding me, right?"

"I'm fine. Nothing bad happened. Just let me tell it before you freak out, okay?" I wait until the panic clears from her face before I continue. "He was a stranger to me, but I was no stranger to him."

"I'm not feeling better about this yet."

"I realized the guy who'd been touching me in...rather intimate ways...wasn't Max, and of course I panicked."

"I can imagine. I'm panicking now."

"I was thinking there was some rapist in my house, and I kneed him in the balls and got the hell out of the bed, but then my phone was dead and I couldn't call for help. And he was trying to get me to calm down and all the sudden he just...stopped." I make myself take a breath. "I wasn't thinking straight, but I think everything changed when he saw my ring."

"A rapist with morals?"

"He was no rapist, Liz. He looked at my hand and then he got dressed—pulled on his shirt and pants. What kind of sex offender strips down to his boxers and climbs into bed to cuddle with his victim half the night?"

"A really screwed-up one?"

"He held me," I murmur into my coffee, "and woke me up with sweet kisses on my neck. He knew my name, knew how I like to be touched. When he saw my ring, he said, 'You could have told me.' Then, before he left, he said he hoped *Max* and I had a nice life—mentioning Max by name."

Lizzy whistles long and low. "He knows about Max?"

I nod and add, "But does Max know about him?" I let that sink in for a minute. "Max is the love of my life. Why would I ruin that?

"Was he hot?"

I roll my eyes. "Yes, but that's hardly the point."

"So who was it? Anyone from town?"

"No one I recognized, but that doesn't mean anything when I can't remember the last year."

"Oh, good point." She sips her coffee. "What did he look like?"

"Young, probably my age. Dark hair, a little shaggy like Max's, I guess. He was tall, built."

"Again, like Max," Liz says.

"Maybe taller than Max and not quite that muscular, but impressive still."

"You're describing half of Max's workout buddies."

"Fuck," I groan. "Please tell me I'm not cheating on him with one of his friends."

"In what ways *didn't* he look like Max?"

"Tattoos!" I hold my hands together. Maybe this will be the piece of information that will help Lizzy identify my visitor. "He had several. Some numbers over his left pec and a Hulk tattoo on his right shoulder."

Lizzy raises a brow. "As in Hulk Hogan?"

"As in the Incredible Hulk. *You won't like me when I'm angry* Hulk."

"You're engaged to Max Hallowell and having an affair with a nerd?"

"Maybe?" I lift my palms helplessly. "Do you know who he is? I'm really freaking out here."

She shakes her head. "Not a clue."

"Stupid amnesia."

"No kidding." She paces. Stops. Paces. Looks out the window, toys with her hair, paces some more. Suddenly, her head pops up, making her curls bounce around her face. "Oh my God. So obvious!"

"What's obvious?" I'm so worried she's going to say, "Tell Max everything." That whole "honesty is the best policy" thing has always worked for me, but...

I'm not sure this is a the-truth-will-set-you-free kind of situation. And...

How can I tell Max the truth when I don't even know what the truth is?

"This is the twenty-first century, right? If you and some guy had a thing, there would be digital evidence."

"Digital evidence? You think I'd have let him take pictures? Oh God! Video?"

Lizzy winces. "Let's hope not, but that's not what I mean. You know, text messages and stuff."

I don't even bother replying because I'm scrambling toward my purse so I can look at my phone.

I scroll through my text messages. A conversation between me and Max, between me and my mom. Maggie, Cally, Lizzy, even Cally's little sister Drew.

"Any nude pics?" Lizzy asks. "Sexting? Anything?"

"There's absolutely nothing here to make me think I was having an affair."

She grabs my phone from my hand and does her own scroll-through. "Maybe the guy's just some nut job," she says, shuddering. "God. I hope he doesn't come back."

"Me too." But even if he is a nut job, that doesn't explain what he knew about me...or the way my chest ached when I watched him leave.

September—Eleven Months Before Accident

The minute I walk into Max Hallowell's health club, I feel like I'm wearing a giant neon sign that says I don't belong here. It's not that I don't work out. Hell, I work out more than most of the skinny girls I know. But I do it in private. At home or in my mom's basement. Never in a downtown health club where everyone can stare at me and wonder how soon I'll give it up and go on a Hostess run. Because that's what people think about fat chicks. They assume we're lazy and don't work out. They assume we eat Little Debbie Cakes three times a day and don't touch fruits or vegetables.

"Hanna!" Max calls from the back. He's squatting as he stacks weights by the chest press. "To what do I owe the honor?"

Returning his smile, I look around but don't see anyone I know. The club is slow right now, only a couple of senior citizens occupying the treadmills on the far side of the room. "I wanted to, um, maybe sign up for personal training."

He pushes off the ground and wipes his hands on his shorts as he crosses to me. His smile is wide and white and so damn sincere I want to melt under it. "Tell me what you have in mind. I'll see who I can hook you up with. I have a couple of female trainers but their specialties are different, so it just depends on what your goals are."

My heart stumbles in my chest from being this close to Max. I have to tilt my chin up just to see his face. "I was hoping you could do it?" It comes out as a question, a far cry from the flirty, suggestive tone Lizzy used when we planned this.

Surprise flashes over his face. "Me? Really?"

"If you can fit me in, that would be my preference." I can't believe this comes as a surprise to him. Women all over town pay to train with Max just so they can admire his body while he puts them through suicide drills. An hour of watching his muscles flex under his T-shirt is enough motivation to do most anything.

"I'd love to train with you. Let's sit down and talk about what you want to accomplish."

He pulls out a stool by the bar, and I climb onto it and cross my legs nervously. He takes the spot next to me.

"Okay." He grabs a notebook and pen from the other side of the bar. "Let's start with long-term goals and break them down to short-term. Where do you see yourself in twelve months?"

Sexy, skinny, and naked in your bed.

"Fitness-wise," he clarifies with a wink.

My cheeks burn as if he can read my thoughts. I tuck my hair behind my ear. I came ready to work out. Kind of. I'd normally wear my hair up to work out, but Lizzy insisted it was sexier to wear it down.

"I'd like to run a half marathon next summer."

Truth is, I have no desire to run a marathon—half or otherwise. I just want to lose weight and get Max to notice me. I exercise regularly, but I hate running with the fiery intensity of a thousand suns. But Max is a runner. He runs all the time, and since this is all about spending time with him, I've decided I'm going to be a runner too.

"That's totally doable." Max writes *Run half marathon* on his notepad. "Are you a runner now or are we starting from scratch?"

"Do I look like a runner?" I regret the question as soon as it's out of my mouth. Lizzy gave me strict instructions to leave my self-deprecating humor at home. She doesn't get that it's a Fat Girl Coping Mechanism. She wouldn't get that. How could she? "Sorry. I mean, I haven't done much running. My mom made me when I was in junior high—a mile every night after school. I hated it. I want to learn to love it—on my terms—but I haven't done much since I started college."

"A year is plenty of time," Max assures me. "I mean, you're obviously fit, so I bet we're still working with a pretty impressive baseline."

Obviously fit? No one has ever said that to me before.

He grins. "Why are you blushing?"

Because you're looking at me. "I guess this is all a little embarrassing."

"Don't be embarrassed," he says. "You know what you want, and I'll make sure you get it."

"I'm going to hold you to that."

Present Day

"I can't wait to get drunk," Lizzy calls from my bathroom, where she's putting on her makeup. "Are you going to get drunk with me or are you still obsessing about calories?"

"I might drink some." I force a smile.

I guess if I'm going to keep the body I spent the last year finding, I'll need to keep some of the new habits Lizzy finds so annoying. But right now I'm too worried about potentially being a cheating bitch to give my habits—new or old—much thought. Anyway, Dr. Perkins seemed to think I shouldn't be counting calories. Though I'm not sure a pitcher of daiquiris is what she had in mind either.

Truth be told, I'm terrified to go to this party. What if I run into Mr. Hulk Tattoo? What if he outs our relationship—or whatever it was—to everyone? But I can't spend the rest of my life hiding in my apartment, so I'm going.

"Is Max coming?"

I shake my head. "He has a late client and can't make it."

Lizzy flips her head upside down and adds some sort of magic curling goo to it. "You know what I'd like?" she asks as she scrunches handfuls of hair.

I plug in my flat iron and lean against the doorframe while I wait for it to warm. "What would you like?"

"One hot fucking night with Nate Crane."

I nearly choke on my tongue laughing. "Asher's rocker friend?"

"What? Maggie has Asher. Why can't I have Nate?" She flips her head back up and wriggles her eyebrows at me. "Tell me you wouldn't sacrifice everything to have a night of dirty, no-holds-barred sex with Mr. Rock God."

I just shrug. "I have Max."

She rolls her eyes. "Right. Max and Mr. Hulk Tattoo, meaning you got more sexy male ass last night than I've had in the last six months. Yet another reason I deserve a night with Crane. I'm the only one around here who isn't getting any."

"Poor thing."

"You have no idea. Max can't keep his hands off you."

I frown at my reflection and run my finger along my newly defined jawline. Max can't keep his hands off me. I wonder if that started before or after I lost the weight.

She digs through my makeup bag. "So any revelations about last night's mystery visitor?"

"None." *Stupid amnesia.*

"Well, I vote that he was some nut job. You should really call the cops. The guy's probably stalking you or something."

"I don't think I want to do that. Not yet."

"But you're going to tell Max, aren't you?"

Anxiety lodges like a wet ball in my throat. "I just want to have more information before I tell him anything."

"Hanna, this is serious. I saw a *60 Minutes* episode once about a guy who imagined he had this whole relationship with the woman he was stalking. He watched her all the time, so in his mind they were together. Then she started dating someone and the dude flipped out and pulled a gun on him."

I turn and she's staring at me, worry in her bright blue eyes. I don't know how to explain to her that my heart told me I could trust this guy. "There's too much we don't know. I don't want to screw things up with Max for nothing. I need to get some facts straight. That's all."

"Okay." Her eyes brim with tears. She lunges forward and wraps her arms around me. "I've missed this."

"What?"

"My sister. I've missed talking about things. Confiding in each other. You have no idea how lonely it's been for me these last few months."

"I hope I never have to find out," I whisper, and she squeezes me even harder.

By the time the party rolls around, I'm already anxious for an excuse to leave. I just want to go home and make out with Max until I'm confident I haven't screwed up a good thing.

It's a hot night, and Lizzy vetoed my jeans and T-shirt for a short denim skirt and halter that look surprisingly impressive on my new body. The halter shows off my sculpted shoulders—apparently I've been lifting weights with Max—and the skirt shows my toned runner's legs. I top the outfit off with strappy black heels and throw my hair in a twist. Despite the bruise on my right arm and the side of my face, I feel so sexy I snap a picture of myself in the mirror and send it to Max with the caption, *Wish you were coming tonight.*

Two minutes later, I'm treated to his reply.

Max: *I don't want to wait any longer than I have to. The club closes at nine. Meet me here.*

His words send hot tingles of nerves and arousal rushing to my center.

Hanna: *It's a date.*

I'm still grinning at my phone when I hear Lizzy whistle. "Damn, girl."

"I know, right? Who knew I could look like this?"

She frowns. "You were sexy before you lost the weight. I was referring to the way you're glowing."

"Oh." I press my phone to my chest. "I hope I didn't screw things up. Max is... He's amazing."

She rolls her eyes. "I'm sure there's a perfectly logical explanation for all of this. Come on. Let's get out of here."

When we walk into Asher's, Maggie greets us at the door in a white sundress and bare feet. "You made it! I'm so glad!"

"We're on a mission." I grin and nod toward Lizzy. "My twin would like to seduce your musician friend."

"You're going to seduce Nate?" Maggie asks, skepticism all over her face.

"Unless you're planning on sharing Asher."

Maggie snorts. "As if. But Nate? Really? The guy sitting in my basement in a Spider-Man shirt?"

Lizzy scoffs. "Have you heard that voice? God concentrated sexiness and gave it to the world through Nate Crane's voice. The boy could melt the panties off a nun."

Maggie rolls her eyes. "I think we all know you're no nun. Come on. Everyone's in the basement."

She leads the way into the house and to the stairs, where she stops and points at a small table. "House rules, no phones or other distracting electronics with the music." She digs her own out of her pocket and tosses it in the basket with the others. Lizzy and I follow suit then head down the stairs to where everyone is milling in the music room. Asher doesn't have big parties. In fact, his parties might better be described as "get-togethers" with most of the attendees being members of my immediate family. Tonight, there are more guests than normal—maybe a dozen total—probably due to his musician friend who's in town.

I look to the stage, where Asher is playing acoustic guitar and singing into a mic connected to a small amp. My gaze shifts to the man sitting next to him and I stop breathing.

"Asher's hot too," Lizzy's assuring Maggie, "but Nate could do *whatever* he wanted to me and I'd thank him in the morning."

Nate Crane. Dark, shaggy hair, deep voice, intense gaze. And no doubt a Hulk tattoo hidden beneath his right sleeve of his Spider-Man T-shirt. "Holy shit."

"He's got a nice voice, doesn't he?" Maggie says.

I nod dumbly. A nice voice that whispered sweet nothings in my ear last night. Hot and dirty sweet nothings.

"You can't go being all star-struck when you're used to Asher hanging around." Maggie nudges me with her elbow. "You've met Nate. You two really hit it off."

"We hit it off? Why would you say that?" It comes out way too defensive, and I have to take a breath and force my shoulders away from my ears.

"He's a friend of Asher's. You kept me company when I went to see Asher and Nate perform in St. Louis a few months ago. God, that must be so weird, not remembering anything."

The guys transition into "Unbreak Me," a song Asher wrote for Maggie.

She bites her lip.

"Go on up there," Liz says. "You don't need to babysit us."

"Thanks." Maggie walks to the front of their makeshift stage and sinks to her haunches.

"Want something to drink?" Liz asks. "Because I'm at least three drinks short of the courage I need to approach that beautiful man up there."

"I'm okay for now."

"If you say so." She points toward the bar. "I'll be over there if you need me."

I nod but I can't take my eyes off the stage—off Nate. They finish the final chords of "Unbreak Me," and everyone applauds as Asher stands and kisses Maggie soundly.

When Asher leaves the stage, Nate stays behind, strumming chords to a song I don't recognize. He lifts his gaze. For five painful beats of my heart, our eyes lock. There's so much in his eyes. Pain, anger, frustration. I see it all there before he refocuses on his fingers and starts to croon the lonely lyrics of his song.

I'm nobody's hero, baby. Try not to fall too deep.
I'm nobody's angel, love, but you were crying in your sleep.
I'm useless, empty, nothing, sugar. Wait around and then you'll see.
You thought you'd find your answers, but now you're lost in me.

The words tap into me, loosening something in my chest until I feel like anyone looking at me can see my confusion and the inexplicable aching of my heart.

And when he lifts his head and watches me as he sings the last verse of his song, I don't move. I don't hide from those eyes that know too much. I don't run from that face that could destroy my whole world. I stand transfixed, the words rolling through my veins like they're part of my blood.

After he strums the final chords, he puts down his guitar and leaves the stage without explanation or promise to return.

My feet are following him before I've decided what to do. He heads up the stairs and out back, through the French doors and onto the patio, where he keeps going until he hits the path in front of the river.

He's trying to escape me. I should be happy, right? The past can stay in the past, and whatever mistake I made with this rocker can be left behind with it. But I can't let him walk away without answers.

"Stop!" I rush down to the river, my heels sinking into the rain-softened earth. "Who are you?"

He turns slowly, the confusion back on his face. "Is that supposed to be funny? Pretending there was nothing between us wasn't enough? You need to pretend you don't even know who I am?"

"I—" Oh my God. The hurt in his eyes. "I *don't* know who you are," I say carefully. "But maybe I should? I was injured and I have amnesia, so I honestly don't know you." And if that doesn't sound like a line from a Lifetime movie, I'm not sure what does.

"Amnesia? You're kidding me."

"I'm not." He starts toward me, and I hold out a hand to stop him. "I'd prefer you to stay over there. Please."

He pulls back, watching me. "Amnesia," he repeats.

"Yeah."

"You don't know who I am." It's not a question—more a realization.

"I don't know who you are or why you would crawl into my bed in the middle of the night. I don't understand why—" My breath catches and fat, hot tears spill onto my cheeks. Suddenly this is just all too much. "I don't understand," I repeat, and leave it at that.

"You don't remember anything? Do you know who you are?"

"Yeah. I remember everything up until about a year ago, but the last eleven months are just…gone."

He drags a hand through his hair, and I'm struck again by how gorgeous he is. Dark messy hair, dark intense eyes. His T-shirt clings to his sculpted arms. Tattoos peek out from the sleeves. No matter how hard I look, I can't remember being with him. So why do I have this feeling in my chest like my heart knows something I don't?

"Do I know you?" I ask.

He lets out a huff and stares at the starlit sky. "Yeah. You do." When he drops his gaze back to meet mine, his eyes are moist with unshed tears. "I'm the idiot who's in love with you."

In love with me? "But I'm engaged."

"I saw that," he whispers, his gaze flicking back to my hand.

"Can I ask? Did that happen before or after the amnesia?"

"Before."

"Fuck." The word isn't screamed or thrown like a stone. He breathes it—exhaling the sound like so much disappointment.

To me, Nate's a stranger, but to him, I'm...*what?*

We just stare at each other, him looking heartbroken and angry, me trying to piece it all together in my head and make some sense of this. I'm engaged to Max Hallowell. I'm not the kind of girl who would get engaged to one guy when she's been sleeping with another.

Am I?

We stand here, the passing seconds measured by the chirp of a lonely tree frog. I scan my mind for anything. A memory, a piece of information, useless trivia—I search for anything at all I can take from my brain to make sense of this illogical ache in my heart.

Finally, he shoves his hands in his pockets and looks out over the water. "I've gotta get out of here, Han."

Han. He knows me. I can feel it. I know him. My heart does, if not my injured brain. "Please, tell me what happened. What did I do?" I whisper. "I don't understand."

He shrugs. "What's there to understand? You're wearing his ring."

Then he walks away, and I'm alone and confused. And I think I have a broken heart, but I don't know if it's breaking for me or for him. And I don't know who did the breaking.

Chapter
SEVEN

WHEN I return to the party, I immediately spot Nate sitting in a chair beside Asher, his guitar in his big hands, his dark hair falling over one eye as he jots notes on a piece of paper. Something twists in my chest at the sight of him. I want to tell myself it's regret or fear—anything but the longing I know it to be.

Maggie and Lizzy motion me over from the bar, but I shake my head and stay by the stairs. As if he senses me, Nate lifts his head and his eyes immediately lock with mine.

I might not understand the tangle of emotions in my chest, but there's no mistaking the anger that flashes over his face when he sees me, and because I'm a coward, I can't face it.

I run back upstairs.

"Where's she going?" I hear Maggie ask.

"She wasn't feeling great," Lizzy says. "I'll check on her."

I'm in the hallway when I feel her behind me, her hand on my shoulder.

"What's wrong?"

Everything. "Nothing. The doctor said the headaches and dizziness might give me a problem for a few days. A party probably wasn't the best idea."

Her expression is more worried than disappointed. "Let me

take you home."

"No. It's a beautiful night, and I'd actually like the fresh air. And I think I'm going to swing by the club and see Max."

"Okay," she whispers. "Promise you'll call me if I can help?"

I take in a long, slow breath. "Go back down there and have a good time."

"Oh, right." Her eyes light up. "I have a rocker to seduce."

My stomach lurches, but I force a smile. "Right."

I watch her go back down before I turn back to the basket of cell phones by the stairs. After shuffling through it, I pull out the few phones I don't recognize as belonging to me or one of my sisters.

I hit the buttons to bring them to life and swipe all three screens to unlock them. One screen, no doubt Asher's, has a picture of Maggie and Zoe as the wallpaper, one has a young woman I don't recognize, and the other has Storm Troopers.

There's no question in my mind that the Storm Trooper phone belongs to the man with the Hulk tattoo and the Spider-Man shirt. The idea of this hard-ass rocker being a closet geek is so adorable. I soften toward him without wanting to.

Before I can think it through, I'm swiping my fingers across the screen and pulling up Nate's text messages. It doesn't take long for me to find a thread with my name.

The last one I sent was the day of my accident.

Hanna: *Left you a message. We need to talk when you get into town.*

What did I want to talk to him about? Was I going to tell him I was marrying Max? I scroll back through some harmless if flirty *Good morning* and *Good to hear your voice tonight* texts before I land on a conversation so damning it makes my hands shake.

The hallway is empty, but I can't risk anyone else seeing these. I take the phone out onto the back patio, sink into a chair, and scroll back to the beginning of the incriminating conversation. I don't take a single breath while I read it.

Nate: *Did you remember to take your gift home with you?*
Hanna: *I did. God knows what airport security thought of it when they searched my bag.*
Nate: *I'm sure they've seen worse. Glad you have it with you.*
Hanna: *It's a sorry substitute for you.*
Nate: *I'll make it up to you when I get to Indiana. I'm coming straight to your place and keeping you in bed for days.*
Hanna: *Hmm. That sounds kind of boring.*
Nate: *Get naked, woman. I want to tell you how to use my gift.*
Hanna: *Bossy.*
Nate: *Only because it makes you wet.*
Hanna: *Naked.*
Nate: *In bed?*
Hanna: *I've been in bed since you first texted. I have a 6 a.m. running date tomorrow.*
Nate: *You should cancel it. I don't want you running off those curves.*
Hanna: *You're the only one who likes my so-called "curves."*
Nate: *Who else matters?*
Hanna: *Good point. I miss your face.*
Nate: *I miss yours too. You know what else I miss?*
Hanna: *Tell me.*
Nate: *The sound you make when I touch your breasts. The feel of your nipples against my tongue. I miss sliding my hand between your legs and finding you wet. I miss the taste of you. The feel of your heels against my back as I take your clit between my lips. But mostly, I miss holding you in my arms. So fucking perfect. So completely mine.*

I don't know what I expected. Maybe it was supposed to be like in the movies, where the amnesia patient sees something from her past and suddenly everything comes flooding back to her. But there's no memory here, and my half of this conversation might as well have been written by another woman.

When I lift my head, Nate is standing in front of me, hands

tucked in his pockets, his eyes bored.

"See anything good?" he asks.

My heart is pounding and my breath is shallow and shaky. My cheeks burn and it has nothing to do with regret or guilt or embarrassment. The things he wrote. The things he said. There's a heavy tightness between my legs. My mind may still be confused, but my body? My body wants Nate as much as it ever wanted Max.

Oh God, Max. *I cheated on Max.* "Why would I risk everything?"

His jaw hardens and he shrugs. "You'd have to ask your fiancé."

"You *know* why I can't do that." I push my chair back, and the scraping of metal against concrete rends the air. I lift my chin. "I want to understand. I need you to talk to me."

He tenses at my demand. "No, I don't."

"You don't understand what this is like. Not remembering? I'm planning a wedding to this man I've wanted most of my life. Don't I owe it to him—don't I owe it to *myself*—to have the truth out there before we promise until death do us part?"

Even in the moonlight, I can see the pain in his eyes.

"I just need answers." I lift my chin and move toward the back wall of the house, toward him. Immediately, I regret the decision because his lips curve into a wicked smile and he closes what distance is left between us. "I need the truth," I whisper weakly.

"The truth? Is that what you really want, angel?" His deep voice dances over my skin like a caress. A little tender. A lot wicked.

I can't reply. I'm too busy holding my breath. Too deep of an inhale might brush my breasts against his chest, and I'm afraid to touch him. Afraid of what it might make me feel.

As if he can read my mind, he takes another step closer, and when I step to the side to turn away, I'm against the wall and his body is against mine, his hot breath at my ear.

"Do you want to know what it was like between us?" he whispers.

"Yes."

I realize my mistake when a groan rumbles from his chest. "Should I start with how wet you were every time I touched you? Or maybe how you begged me that first night?"

"I didn't."

"Have you been telling yourself some wicked rocker seduced you? That I tricked you into my bed? Sorry. You asked for the truth. You begged. Right there outside the club, you begged me until I ripped your panties off and you were too busy biting my neck to talk anymore. Is that what you're hoping to remember? How you wanted me so badly you let me finger you out in the open, against that building where anyone could have seen?"

My breathing is uneven, my cheeks hot. When I press into his chest to put some distance between us, my traitorous hands curl into his shirt instead.

He makes a low growling sound at the back of his throat. His teeth nip at my earlobe. Lightning cracks in the sky behind him. "You might have forgotten me, but you still like dirty talk, don't you? And maybe if I made you come now, you'd still scream my name. Because you always screamed *my* name, Hanna. Never his."

I gasp. "You are horrible."

"What are you really upset about? That you wanted me? Or that even as you stand here wearing his ring, you're secretly hoping I'll tell you about it. Secretly wishing you could remember all the details."

"I don't," I bite out, the words edged with the sob I'm holding back. I shove him, and he steps away, but not because I'm strong enough to move him. I know better. But he steps back. He gives me that.

My legs are weak and I have to steady myself against the wall. I betrayed Max. Emotion riots in my chest, too much to contain. The worst is true. But the ache of arousal between my legs—that's the worst betrayal of all.

"Tell me why I did it," I say. "I need to understand."

He shoves his hands into his pockets and looks out toward the fenced area behind the patio, where Asher's hot tub gurgles as it spills into the pool. "I made you a promise," he says, his words measured. "I promised that when you made your decision, I would respect it. That if you took his ring, I wouldn't try to change your mind."

Seconds ago, I wanted his knowing eyes anywhere but mine,

but now I wish he would look at me. I need to see the eyes of the man I feel this inexplicable connection to. The man I was considering leaving my fiancé for.

"I always knew you deserved better than me." His voice is a deep rumble that tries to hide behind the distant thunder. "I hope he's worthy of you. I sure as fuck wasn't."

Finally, he turns to me and takes my hands into his. His mouth is inches from mine, and his gaze rests on my lips. I wait for his kiss—wonder if I want it. Time snags on my indecision. Trips. Stutters. Slows to a crawl.

Lifting one finger at a time, he removes his cell phone from my grasp then steps away. He disappears into the darkness, his silence a promise I can't remember him making and the ache in my chest a regret I don't understand.

I walk around the side of the house, and drizzle fills the air and hits my hot cheeks. When it grows heavier, changing to rain, I don't run for shelter. Pausing, I look up into the dark, moonless night and let the rain shower my fears.

I'm soaking wet by the time I get to the gym, and when I push through the double doors, Max is squatting in front of a leggy blonde, his hand curled around her thigh. It's nearly nine p.m., and they're the only two here.

"Take it deeper," he says, his voice rough. "Yeah…just like that. Now really squeeze. Now go again."

The girl adjusts the weights on her shoulders and drops into a low lunge. "That *hurts*," she whines.

"Again," Max says. He turns his head toward the door—and me—and his face lights up. "Ten more on that side," he tells the girl. Then he's coming over to me.

"Sorry I'm early."

He doesn't look upset about it, and I can only hope he's not. After talking to Nate, I'm desperate to see Max again, to reassure myself that I haven't lost him. Whatever I've done, if he wants me, if he loves me, we can get through this. Can't we?

"No apology necessary." He runs his gaze over me and his nostrils flare. He laces a finger through one of the belt loops on my jean skirt and tugs me close. "Even hotter in person," he murmurs against my ear. "Did you walk through the rain just to make me crazy with wanting you?"

I bite my lip. I didn't give thought to anything other than getting away from the party.

"What now?" the girl whines.

He nips at my earlobe—the same earlobe Nate Crane just bit—and shame rushes through me in a tremor. Max misunderstands my tremble and whispers, "Soon," before pulling away and turning back to his client. "Other side."

The girl whimpers. Actually *whimpers*. "At this rate, I'm not going to be able to walk out of here."

"You said you wanted to be sore tomorrow." He cuts his eyes to me and winks before returning his attention to the girl. "I aim to please."

The girl flashes him a disappointed look, and I have to bite back my laughter. I'm sure she said that, and I'm sure she had a very different scenario in mind. I wonder if this is the first time a guy has ever turned her down.

"This is my fiancée," Max says, wrapping an arm around my waist. "She's just here to use the steam room."

"I am?"

"The cleaning crew just left, so it should be good as new." He drops his head until his mouth hovers right over my ear and whispers, "I'll meet you in there after I lock up."

Meet me? My heart kicks up a notch, as if I'm the one doing the lunges. "Oh…"

"Come on," he tells the blonde. "You can go deeper than that."

I slip past them and to the door that reads *Ladies' Locker Room*. Max's gym is nice. Clean and shining, well maintained. I don't remember working out here before, but Lizzy told me I'd become quite the gym rat in the last eleven months.

The locker room is large. One wall is covered by a mirror over three sinks. The other has a couple dozen wooden lockers. I drop my purse on the bench by the lockers and follow the hall back.

There are three showers, all clean, with white towels folded on racks between them. Beyond the showers is the steam room. I hear the hiss of the steam before I see it.

I pull open the foggy glass door and am hit by a hot puff of steam. Biting my lip, I scan the tile walls, the chairs, and the two-tiered bench along the back wall. He wants me to wait in here for him. Is this something we do a lot?

I have to let out a slow breath as my imagination runs wild at the idea of waiting here naked for Max. Or better, Max joining me naked.

He's going to expect me to have sex. I mean, of course—that only makes sense. Engaged couples have sex. I'm nervous. No, I'm terrified. No matter how many times I had sex in the last months, I don't remember it, so I might as well still be the virgin I was at the time of my last memory.

After talking to Nate tonight, I'm not worried he'll be bothering me or running to Max. I should be happy. My secret is safe, and I can focus on my upcoming marriage.

So why does the idea of having sex with my fiancé feel like cheating?

Pushing aside the thought, I go back to the lockers to strip out of my clothes. A towel secured under my arms, I return to the steam room and step in this time.

Sinking into a chair, I lean back and close my eyes as the heat relaxes my muscles and quiets my mind.

I drift off to sleep, and just as my dreams tug me under, my mind skates along the edge of a memory—Max and me in the gym before we started dating. I asked him to be my trainer. It's there, a memory as clear as the ones I never lost, and I wrap myself in the comfort of it. Me. Max. No affairs. No angry rockers with broken hearts.

"Hey, sleeping beauty," someone whispers in my ear.

My muscles are so relaxed, I don't want to move. I stretch my arms and legs, and my towel falls to my waist as I open my eyes.

"Oh, damn, Hanna." Max stands before me, his chest bare, a towel tied around his hips. I can't quite make out his face in the steam, but I don't need to see his expression to know he wants me.

Desire radiates off every water molecule in the room—a breath held and waiting for release.

I extend my stretch, arching my back in a move that thrusts my breasts toward him.

"Sorry it took me longer than I expected." His voice sounds strained as he offers his hand. "I had a new client come in just as I was trying to lock up."

I take his hand and stand, but when I reach to grab my fallen towel, he holds me fast.

"Please don't," he says.

Maybe I'd be self-conscious in another setting, but here in the steam, I turn sexy and wanton under his gaze. I feel nothing but determination under the weight of the unwanted ache in my heart while talking to Nate. Determination to prove to myself that *this* is the man I love—no one else.

With that first recovered memory in my grasp, I'm hopeful for the first time in days. I drop my gaze to his towel and arch a brow. "I sense a double standard."

He groans and drops his mouth to mine. His kiss is long and slow and thorough. He tastes like cinnamon gum and strokes his tongue against mine as he cups my breast in his hand.

"I believe it's my turn to touch you," he whispers against my lips. His thumb rolls over my nipple in the slow, sensuous motion of a man who plans to take his time. "And touching you in here ranks high on my list of fantasies."

I curl my nails into his back and nip at his bottom lip. Because I don't want him to take his time. I want him to touch me and kiss me until I've forgotten the sound of Nate's voice, until I'm so sure of our love and our future that my anxiety fades.

With his free hand, Max cups my other breast and treats it to the same slow torture.

"Max," I whimper, arching toward him, wanting more.

"How was the party?"

"What?"

His lips curl into a smile. "God, I love that I can make you lose your mind like that."

I slide my hands into his hair. "You can. You do."

Trailing kisses down my neck and over my collarbone, he makes his way to my breast and opens his mouth over my nipple. Slow, steady, achingly meticulous, he circles it with his tongue before pulling it into his mouth. My breasts grow heavier with every stroke of his tongue, the ache between my thighs more insistent. The steam has set my senses on fire, and the brush of his knuckles down my side is as thrilling as the first time a boy went up my shirt.

Just when I think I'm going to have to beg for more, he takes my nipple into his mouth and sucks—long and hard. My knees go weak and he has to hold me tight as I slip in his arms.

"Come over here," he murmurs. He leads me to the tiered benches and takes a seat on the bottom row. His erection is thick and tall under the towel, but when I reach to uncover it, he stops my hand. "Leave it. You tempt me too much."

"But I like touching you," I object.

"You like making me lose my mind."

A giggle slips from my lips. "It's a nice feeling."

"Come here." He tugs me forward until I'm straddling him, the hard length of his cock needy and glorious between my legs. As he returns his mouth to my breasts, sucking and licking in turn, I rock against him. My thighs squeeze him as the sensation of his mouth on my breasts mixes with the pressure of his erection through the towel.

His hands slide around me and over my ass, kneading the flesh of my cheeks as his mouth works at my breasts.

Whimpering, I arch my back and shift my hips just so, and suddenly pleasure snaps through me like a whip. My hips want to rock, to circle, to grind against his length, but I force them to still.

"Move against me," he commands. "I want to feel you move."

The friction of the towel against my swollen clit is almost too much, almost uncomfortable, but it's a good kind of discomfort, and his cock swells bigger and more insistent between my thighs. I don't know if I could stop if I wanted to. Unless it was for something different. Something *more*. How easy would it be for him to move this towel and slide into me right now? My fear is gone, replaced by red-hot aching need. Doesn't he want it as much as I do? Maybe he doesn't have protection with him.

I can't think on the question for long before his hand is back at my breast, kneading and massaging. It takes my breath. Then he sucks me hard and mercilessly into his mouth and I buck against him. I circle my hips and rock, circle and rock. I'm so close to that edge, and as much as my body begs to slide over it, I don't want this to end.

Max grips my hip and rises off the bench to add another ounce of pressure between my legs. I cry out. In pleasure. In frustration. I need more.

"Please." My plea echoes against the walls.

He shifts us so quickly that he's moved me before I know what's happening. He lifts me onto the higher bench. I immediately miss the promise of him between my legs.

He sinks down as he spreads me open with a hand against each thigh. Then I'm open and exposed to him and his lips are close, the hot steam and his breath mingling and sweeping over my sensitive sex.

At first, his touch is tentative, his fingers tracing my folds before dipping into me. I bite my lip to hold back my cry, but then he lowers his mouth and wraps his lips around my clit at the same moment he slides two fingers inside me, demanding more with his touch. His fingers pump as his tongue strokes. Hungry, greedy.

Then, when I'm so full of tight-winding pleasure that I think I need to pull back, he takes my ankle and props my foot on the bench beside my hip. I'm stretched open and his fingers curl and coax and his lips wrap around my clit, and I can't stop myself from rocking into his face, fucking his fingers the way I want him to fuck me. I can't hold on anymore. I'm flying, falling, disintegrating until I'm nothing but the hot steam around us.

Chapter
EIGHT

I'M CURLED up against Max as he traces my spine with his fingertips and presses kisses along my hairline.

"Do we do this a lot?" I murmur against his chest.

He laughs, a silent chuckle I can feel more than hear. "Which part?"

"The steam room?"

"Never before, but I think we will now. In fact, I think I'll save my pennies so we can get one installed in our future home."

"Our home," I say, testing the words. "I like the sound of that."

"Me too." His voice is hoarse.

"Where will we live after we get married?"

"We hadn't really talked about it, but if it's between my tiny apartment above the club and your tiny apartment above the bakery, we should probably go with your place."

I frown. "I thought you had a house?" Not that I remember ever being there, but I remember seeing him work in the lawn of a tiny ranch off Main.

"I sold it. I was never there anyway." He tucks my hair behind my ear and cups my face in his hand. "I can't give you anything fancy yet, but I will. Whatever you want. I'll make it happen."

"I don't need fancy. Just you."

He wraps his arms around me and squeezes. "We should get out of here."

"Yeah, I think I'm out of sweat."

I grab my towel off the floor, but it's soaked and useless for drying me off. Max opens the door, and a shiver runs through me as the cool air hits my warm skin. He grabs a towel from the stand and wraps it around me.

His clothes are draped over a chair outside the steam room, and as he removes his towel, I can't help but let my eyes slide over his body, every inch of it toned and muscular. There's a three-inch tattoo of a dragon right inside the V of his hipbones. It must have been covered by his shirt when he was in my apartment last night. I want to lick it.

"You have a tattoo."

"I do."

"When did you get it?"

"Last December. I'd been thinking about it for a while, but you talked me into it."

I grin as I skim my fingers over it.

He releases a deep groan. "Hanna, you touch me like that and we won't make it out of here tonight."

I wrap my arms around his neck and rise onto my toes to kiss him. "Max Hallowell, I don't know how I landed a guy like you, but I promise I'm going to be the best wife you could ask for. I'm going to earn this."

Something flashes across his face—sadness, regret?—and he strokes his thumb down my cheek before gathering me against his chest and drawing in a deep breath against my hair.

"I'm the one who needs to earn this. Don't be fooled."

November—Nine Months Before Accident

The morning light reflecting off the river is quickly becoming one of my favorite sights. Even when the ground is covered with a thin sheet of snow and the air is cold enough that I can see my breath, I'm learning to like this time. I can't exactly say I love running, but I appreciate it, and I'm surprised how quickly I'm gaining stamina.

Max climbs out of his car, looking downright edible in his black, long-sleeved, moisture-wicking shirt and shorts. "Good morning!"

"It's a beautiful one," I call back. His smile warms me more than a cloudless spring day. I've become spoiled by this time with him, his attention on me.

We start jogging without preamble. At first I feel really good, but within less than fifteen minutes, my head gets fuzzy and my vision starts to blur.

My feet scuff the ground as I stumble mid-stride. Max grabs my arm and catches me before I can fall.

"Whoa, careful," he murmurs. "Easy there. Are you okay?"

The world spins off-kilter before righting itself, and I point to the ground. "I think I just need to sit down for a minute." I sink to the cold grass, the frozen earth solid and reassuring under me, and try to blink away a sudden wave of nausea.

"Hanna." Max squats before me and cups my face in his hand. Worry creases his brow. "Did you eat this morning?"

I blink. He's touching me, and I don't want to talk about my diet. I want to melt into his warmth. "I don't like to eat before I run," I admit.

"Okay, my lecture on that aside. What about last night?"

"Chicken breast," I answer, mentally amending *half* a chicken breast.

"What else?"

"What do you mean?"

"What did you eat with it?" His thumb strokes my cheek.

"Oh. I had it on about two cups of mixed greens."

"Any starch? Grains? Fruit?"

"No."

He takes a seat next to me and rests his forearms on his knees. "Lunch?"

"I don't know. I was busy. Maybe an apple."

He bows his head. "I'm the worst trainer ever. You didn't say anything about weight loss, and I just assumed you weren't looking to lose weight. But I should have known."

"Known what?"

He smiles at me. "You're just that kind of personality. You know? You decide you're going to do something and you go all in."

"You make it sound like a bad thing."

He grins. "It's not, but you can't starve yourself. If you really want to lose weight, that's okay, but you have to eat to lose."

I try not to roll my eyes at the advice I've heard again and again. I push myself off the ground. "I think I should just go home."

"Hanna, just promise me you'll start eating."

So I can stay this size forever? "Sure."

"Good. Then you can come with me to dinner on Friday."

Frowning, I turn back to him. "Why?"

He stands and brushes off his shorts. "I think it's called a date. I buy you dinner. We eat together. Maybe hold hands on the way home?"

I blink at him and the world spins in front of me again, but I soften my knees and draw in a long, slow breath. "That sounds nice."

"Pick you up at six."

Present Day

Liz: *Nate disappeared, so no sexy rocker for me tonight. Damn. I've known nuns who got more action than I've seen lately.*

I grimace at Lizzy's text from last night. On the one hand, she makes me laugh, but on the other, I don't know what she's going to think when I tell her *Nate* is Mr. Hulk Tattoo.

I'm supposed to spend the day looking at wedding venues with my mom, and all I can think about is whether I cheated on my fiancé. Call me crazy, but I'm pretty sure I need to know if I'm fucking some rock star behind Max's back before I can choose the length of my veil.

I've been working in the bakery since four thirty this morning, and the clock reads twenty to six when Lizzy comes through the front door, her eyes half closed.

"Why couldn't your dream career have required me to sleep past ten every day, huh?" She pushes past me and to the coffee. "I swear, if I weren't an unemployed loser, I'd tell you to find someone else to wake up at the ass crack of dawn." She pours herself a cup of coffee and then dumps cream in it before taking a long drink. "Fuck me, that's good." When she finally opens her eyes and looks at me—really looks at me—she frowns. "What's wrong?"

"I know who Mr. Hulk Tattoo is," I whisper.

She straightens. "Really? Did he come back? Did you see him somewhere?"

"He was at Asher's last night."

She grins. "Oh, the plot thickens!"

"It's Nate Crane, Liz."

"What's Nate Crane?"

"Nate Crane is the guy who got into my bed like he belonged there. He's the guy I was cheating on Max with."

She squeezes her eyes shut and mutters, "God, you're such a bitch."

"What?"

"You're engaged. Sue me for hating you a little. You get the perfect life and the hottie on the side."

"The hottie on the side might ruin the perfect life!" As much as I want to tell myself that my secret was safe, as much as I want to let go of what might or might not have happened with Nate, I can't stop obsessing over what I've done. What if my memories don't return? I need answers.

Liz frowns. "Yeah. I guess you're right. But come on. Who could blame you? Nate. Fucking. Crane. You were fucking Nate Crane."

"We don't know that for sure," I protest.

She cocks her head. "How familiar was he with your body when he was touching you in the dark?"

I wince. "This sucks."

She shakes her head as if still trying to clear away sleepiness. "Okay, so you saw him at the party and realized he was the guy. Then what? Did he approach you?"

"No. The opposite. He saw me and went in the other direction. But this is my life, you know? My future with this *really great guy*. And the more time I spend with Max, the more sure I am that he's the right guy for me, and I don't want to screw this up, but maybe I already have. So I followed Nate outside and told him I have amnesia and he asked when the engagement happened— before or after the amnesia, as if that made a difference—and I told him before and he was upset all over again and wouldn't talk to me about it. He walked away without answering any of my questions, but I got a hold of his cell phone and read through some of our texts to each other, and it looks really bad, and now I don't know who to talk to or where to get answers, but I'm scared I'll lose Max if I tell him and…" I take a long, gasping breath. "Help."

"Okay." She sets her coffee on the counter and comes over to put her hands on my shoulders. "This is going to be all right. We're going to figure this out. Together. But first you have to breathe."

"Right." I draw in another shaky breath. And another. I'm on my third before Lizzy's nodding and smiling.

"Okay. Now do you think you and Nate were just…"

"Just what?"

"Do you think he just came by for booty calls, or do you think you had a relationship?"

"He said, 'I'm the idiot who's in love with you.' Those were his words, 'the idiot who's in love with you.' And then the text messages…?"

"Dirty?"

I nod. "Really dirty."

"Oh, damn, girl."

"I know. Right?"

She rubs her hands together. "Okay. I could talk to Nate, right? Feel him out?"

"He's hella pissed at me, Liz. I don't think he's any more likely to talk to you."

"What about Asher?" she asks, but my horror must be evident on my face because she says, "Okay, okay, bad idea. No one else needs to know until they need to know, right?"

"That's what I'm hoping."

"Your phone!" she exclaims. "We didn't know who we were looking for yesterday! Look in your contacts first. Maybe you have his name programmed as something else."

I scroll through my contacts until I see find his name staring back at me. "He's here. Programmed into my phone."

She makes a hurry-up gesture with her hand. "Well, click on the history."

I frown. I called him last Friday. That was the day of my accident. We had a three-minute conversation. About what? Judging from his reaction when he saw my ring, I obviously wasn't telling him about my engagement.

"Oh, hell, Liz. This doesn't make any sense."

She snatches the phone from my hand and starts scrolling through the history under Nate's contact info. "But you said there were texts from you on his phone?"

"Yeah. A lot of them. I didn't get very far back before he found me and took it back."

"But there's nothing on your phone, which seems to indicate you deleted the evidence."

I cross my arms. "It looks like it."

"Where's your laptop?"

"In the kitchen. I need to—"

I don't get a chance to finish before she darts to the back of the kitchen and opens my laptop. "What's your password?"

I shrug. "That's what I was trying to say. I haven't been able to get on because I don't know. Thank God my calendar is synched with my phone, but I brought it down today because I need to take it to the shop. I can't access my files."

"What have you tried?"

"All the usual passwords I've always used. Birthday, initials, HanHan, initials and birthday together."

"What about your anniversary with Max?"

I lift my palms. "No go."

"What about Nate? Or Nate Crane?"

"That's not it."

"You sure?"

I drop my gaze to the floor. "I tried this morning."

"Or..." She taps on the keyboard for a minute then presses ENTER. The computer beeps at her and gives her the "Wrong Password" warning message. "Hmm." She taps again.

"Let it go, Liz. I've tried."

She hits ENTER and the computer brightens as my desktop appears.

"What was it?"

"'Lost In Me.'" She forces a smile. "But that doesn't mean anything. It's a seriously popular song."

Maybe it's not incriminating evidence, but it doesn't look good either. "Go to my email first."

She opens the email client and loads the "Sent" folder. A quick scroll through shows messages from me to several potential clients, vendors, future brides. When she pulls up my contact list, Nate's name and email are listed, but a search for his email address gives us nothing from the history.

"Why would I have him in my contacts if I've never actually contacted him?"

"Let's check the trash," she says, moving the mouse to pull up the deleted messages. She looks at me. "Empty."

My stomach churns, bile crawling up my throat. "I've never been good about clearing that stuff. Why would I do it here?"

"Because you were trying to hide something?"

"That's what I'm afraid of," I mutter.

A search of my Facebook profile yields similar results. Nate is in my friends list, but we can't find any evidence of correspondence between us. Of course, if we'd been having an affair, I can't believe I'd be stupid enough to flaunt it on Facebook. *Hanna is in a secret mostly-just-about-sex relationship with Nate Crane.* I'm pretty sure they don't have that option yet.

I want to scream. "I wish I were the kind of girl who kept a diary."

"What are you ladies doing?"

I jump at the question and turn to see Drew entering the kitchen from the back door. She's gorgeous, a younger, more petite version of Cally's dark hair and sultry curves. But she's certainly not dressed to impress anyone in her torn-up old jeans and raggedy T-shirt.

"Drew! Good morning!"

"Eh. If you say so. Coffee?"

"Up front," I say just as the bell at the front rings to let us know a customer came in. "And can you get that customer while you're at it?"

"Sure. I'm *great* with the public," she enthuses, with an eye roll thrown in for good measure.

I ignore her sarcasm. "Thanks, Drew," I say, and watch her push through the swinging door to the front of the shop.

"Let's think about this," Lizzy says. "Maggie says you met Nate three months ago at a show in St. Louis. That's also around the time you stopped *trying* to lose weight and started taking drastic measures to *be sure* you lost weight."

"Drastic measures?" Maybe the anorexia I was secretly seeing Dr. Perkins for wasn't much of a secret at all.

"You stopped eating, took your one-a-day workouts to two or three times a day. *Drastic*. That's also when you started pulling away from me."

The truth is that my anorexia is more believable to me than the idea of pulling away from Liz. "You think I did that because of Nate?"

"I didn't say that. I just think *something* happened three months ago and you changed." Her eyes light up and she's back at the computer, pulling up the web browser and typing madly.

"What?"

"Gossip sites." Lizzy's eyes scan the screen as she scrolls down with her mouse. "They're in love with Nate Crane for the obvious reasons, and I bet there's at least one pic of him while he was in St. Louis." She stops scrolling and her shoulders sag.

"What?" I step behind her to see what she found. She minimizes the window, but not before I see the headline.

The thing about being overweight, for me at least, is that I've spent most of my life strategically planning how I'm going to lose weight and change my body. Most fat girls don't like their pictures taken because they truly believe that soon enough they will be smaller, fitter, more toned—more aesthetically pleasing. No matter that I've been overweight my whole life. I wasted so much time and energy thinking about how to get rid of the weight that I never accepted my size.

Fitness people would probably say that's good. They would probably talk about the dangers of complacency and "giving up," blah blah blah. But they don't understand that always hating your size, always planning to change, translates way too easily to self-loathing and depression. And every time someone takes a picture of a fat girl, revealing her true fat-girl form, it feels like an insult, an intentional jab.

But one hundred times worse than the pictures is the commentary, as if we must be *reminded* of this completely unacceptable shortcoming. As if we don't spend the majority of our waking moments thinking about it.

My eyes sting as I blink at the screen where the picture was. Where the headline was.

"They don't know what they're talking about," Lizzy says. "They're fucking shallow idiots."

"Pull it back up, Liz."

She shakes her head. "No. It's stupid. Looking at it is only going to hurt you."

"Pull it back up." My determination must be clear in my voice, because she sighs and clicks on the icon. The browser pops back up on the screen.

The image shows Nate kissing a woman, his hand halfway up the black skirt that's creeping up and exposing her thick thigh. My face is obscured, but there's no doubt in my mind that I'm the woman in the picture under the soul-scarring headline: *Nate Crane's Secret Fatty Fetish.*

I reach over Lizzy and scroll down to the text of the article—a bunch of nothing trying to make legitimate journalism out of spotting Nate making out with an overweight woman outside a St. Louis nightclub. There's no mention of who the woman in the picture is—as if identity is irrelevant—and no mention of what Nate and the girl did before or after making out outside the nightclub. But Nate's words echo in my head.

"You begged. Right there outside the club, you begged me until I ripped your panties off and you were too busy biting my neck to talk anymore. Is that what you're hoping to remember? How you wanted me so badly you let me finger you out in the open, against that building where anyone could have seen?"

He wasn't lying about that. The evidence is right in front of me.

"Do you think I saw this?" I ask Liz.

She chews on her lower lip and shrugs. "It would explain your drastic diet changes."

"It doesn't answer any of my questions, though. Like why would I cheat on Max and how far did it go and…what the hell am I going to do?"

"We'll figure this out. Let me think. Three months ago seems to be when everything changed. That was our graduation, the night you met Nate, and—"

"She started taking those out-of-town baking gigs three months ago."

Lizzy and I turn toward Drew in unison as she pushes back into the kitchen, coffee in one hand, chocolate croissant in the other.

"That was even before this place was opened, but you were doing side gigs for people."

Lizzy's eyes are wide, her fingertips to her mouth. "I didn't even think of that. I found it weird at the time, but I was kind of pissed at you for dropping me. I didn't really give it much thought beyond that it was yet another reason you were better than me."

"I'm not better than you. I'm sorry if I made you feel that way."

She waves away my apology.

"Where was I going?" I ask Drew.

"Different cities," she says around a mouthful of croissant. "I bet you can find your flight information in your email."

Lizzy's already tapping at the keyboard, pulling up my travel folder in my email client. "Bingo."

I scan the destinations from the subject line. "LA, Seattle, New

Orleans."

Lizzy opens a new tab and searches *Nate Crane tour schedule.* She clicks through a link and pulls up the calendar on his website. "The dates and cities of your gigs all line up with Nate Crane performances."

I step back and press my head against the wall before sinking to the floor. "Liz. What have I done?"

Chapter
NINE

"OH, CRAP, Liz! I need to get a shower and get dressed. I have a cake consult in fifteen minutes."

Lizzy arches a brow. "I think Cally will forgive you if you aren't looking your best."

"Not Cally," I say, grabbing my keys. "A wedding cake consultation."

Lizzy grins. "With Cally and William."

My jaw drops and my eyes water. Will and Cally visited me in the hospital. Cally even gushed over my engagement ring, but I didn't notice she was wearing a ring too. "That's…wonderful."

The bell rings, and Drew calls from the front, "Hanna, my sister is here!"

I rush through the swinging door without a word to Lizzy and practically tackle Cally into a hug. "Congratulations!" I screech.

Cally gives me a squeeze before stepping back and frowning.

"On your engagement," Lizzy explains behind me. "She didn't know."

"Oh!" Cally throws her hand over her mouth, and I see her sparkling ring. "Of course she didn't!"

"How did I miss that when you visited me at the hospital?" I take her hand and study the ring. "God, it's gorgeous."

"I didn't have it on that day. The jeweler needed it so he could design my wedding band."

"Wedding band." I melt a little. William and Cally had to go through so much to get this far, and I can't think of any two people who deserve happiness more. "I'm so happy for you."

"Well, I'd hope so. You're in the wedding."

"Ooh!" My eyes fill with tears all over again.

Behind me, Drew grunts, and I can practically *hear* her rolling her eyes. "This would be so sweet if you hadn't already been through it all months ago. Seriously, it's the Twilight Zone around here."

"Come on." I wave Cally over to a table in the corner. "Let's talk about your wedding cake."

December—Eight Months Before Accident

Skinny chicks should be required to take a class in empathy. I'd call it Fat Girl 101 and I'd teach them all the secret rules fat girls live by:

1) Never use the word *fat*. It makes the skinny folk uncomfortable.

2) Pretend to be at peace with your body and size while simultaneously and continuously making your best efforts to reduce it to something more aesthetically pleasing.

3) Pretend to be attracted to the guys you stand a chance with and hide your attraction to The Unattainables.

I've spent most of my life following these simple rules, but tonight they're not coming easily.

I don't want to be *that girl*. The one who can't enjoy herself because she's too busy looking at how much thinner, prettier, or more fashionable the women around her are. The one who can't believe the man on her arm wants to be with her, so she spends all her energy feeding her jealousy toward the women he *should* want. But tonight, I'm all that and worse.

The gallery's winter opening is bustling, and William and

Cally are glowing as people circulate through the new exhibit. Cally waves at me from across the room, her smile bright. Max and I are supposed to go out with them tonight after the opening, but Lizzy's here in a red dress that shows off her long legs and skinny arms, and all I can think about is how inadequate I am.

I'm about to smack myself.

I beeline for the bar and hand a ten to the bartender. "Your biggest glass of your sweetest red, please."

The bartender's eyes drop to my cleavage for a minute, and I actually smile. I forget how much men like tits. I forget that some men like tits enough to overlook everything else. And maybe I should be offended by this stranger's not-so-subtle appreciation of mine, but politically correct or not, knowing that he's looking seriously lifts my spirits.

I take a long pull off the wine and lean on the bar as I scan the room for Max.

"Waiting for your date?" the bartender asks. He's cute. Probably a student at Sinclair like me. He's got that disheveled surfer-boy look going on, even in his white button-up shirt and dress pants.

I take another healthy swallow. Wine goes a long way to make me forget my insecurities, and if I don't want to be *that girl,* I'm gonna need a vat of it tonight. "I am," I say with a sigh. "But last time I saw him, he was checking out my twin."

The surfer boy coughs and pulls at the neck of his dress shirt. He's so obviously uncomfortable in it, I almost feel bad for him. As if giving up, he unbuttons the top button. His eyes dip to my cleavage again, but he pulls them back up so fast it doesn't feel smarmy, just flattering and adorable.

"You have a twin?"

I roll my eyes. Boys and their twin fantasies. Seriously. "Yes, but we're not identical." *Not by a long shot.*

God, if Max had known I was behind him, he never would have checked out Lizzy like that. He's not an asshole or anything. He's just a normal guy. And like any normal guy, he wants to fuck my twin more than he'll ever want to fuck me.

Three dates and he hasn't kissed me. Sure, he's held my hand, hugged me, kissed my cheek. But in three dates, his lips haven't touched mine. That wouldn't be the case if he'd had those three dates with Liz.

"Gah!" I growl. There may not be enough wine or cute-surfer-boy-tit-gawking to ever obliterate this mood.

The surfer boy's brows shoot up. "What?"

"I'm instituting my own drinking game." I prop both elbows on the counter and lean forward, grinning at my own clever idea. "Every time I feel sorry for myself because my date secretly has the hots for my sister, I'm taking a drink."

He shifts behind the counter and refills my wine without me asking. "Can I ask you a question?"

Max appears on the other side of the room and pulls William into one of those male-certified one-armed hugs. They're such a handsome duo—Will with his crazy blond curls, Max with his dark mop, both sporting bodies that belong in men's fitness magazines. Max looks amazing tonight in his pressed slacks and dark blue oxford. Flipping gorgeous and way out of my league. *Drink.* "Ask away," I say behind my wine glass.

"If he's into your sister, why are you with him? Why not be into a guy who's into *you*?"

Because guys aren't into me. Oh, shit. There I go again. *Drink.*

"I mean, if *I* were your boyfriend, for example, I wouldn't care what your sister looks like. Look at you."

I blink at him. Then it occurs to me that the wine is going to my brain. This guy is probably just trying to make me feel better. *Drink.* "I fell for Max when I was thirteen," I confess. "He smiled at me and I…" I take another drink. Really, if I'm going to tell him the story, he should save us both the trouble and hand me the bottle.

"Well, if you decide you want a date who's only interested in you…" He walks around the bar and takes the phone from my fingers to tap on the screen.

I have to smile at him. It's been a long time since someone has gone this much out of his way to make me feel better. "You're really sweet, you know that?"

This time when his eyes drop to my breasts, they slide right down on past to my hips and then linger. "For those curves, I'll be whatever you want me to be."

"Who's this?"

I jump at the sound of Max's voice then back a step away from surfer boy, as if I've just been caught doing something wrong. "Oh, this is Max, my date," I tell the bartender. I widen my eyes and hope he can see the desperate *Please don't tell him what we were talking about* message in my eyes. "Max, this is the bartender, um…"

"Jimmy," the surfer boy replies. He's not bothered in the slightest by Max's presence. He winks at me like we have some sexy secret.

Max takes my hand and squeezes my fingers. "Will you come with me, please?"

I stop trying to figure out Jimmy's odd interest with me and look up at Max. "Sure."

He leads me through the gallery, nearly dragging me along behind his long strides. He takes the stairs two at a time to the loft, where there's a kitchenette and reception area.

When he finally stops and turns to me, I frown. "What's going on?"

"Let me take that." He takes the wine from my hand and sets it on the counter.

"Why?"

"Because I want your hands to be free when I do this."

And that's when it happens. He slides his hands into my hair and sweeps his lips over mine. But this is different than the chaste kisses we've shared before now. This is a hot *sweep, sweep, linger* that promises more. His thumb grazes the line of my jaw, and I open instinctively under him until he's kissing me full-on, his tongue against mine, his lips patient then coaxing, his fingers brushing up my neck and into my hair.

I've waited for this kiss since I was old enough to think kisses from boys were something worth wanting. I've waited for Max since I realized *boys* were worth wanting. And here he is. Kissing me as if he's craved me as long as I've craved him.

Slowly, he leaves my mouth and trails sweet kisses along my jaw and down my neck until his mouth opens against that tender skin at the crook of my neck. His hot tongue sweeps over it.

I close my eyes and try to catch my breath. But it's hard when he's this close and his mouth and teeth and tongue are doing things to my neck that feel so good my brain is imagining them everywhere else. Imagining them places I've never felt a man's tongue.

When he lifts his head, his blue eyes have gone smoky.

"What was that for?" I whisper.

"I think William's bartender was trying to steal away my date."

A puff of air slips between my lips. "He was just trying to cheer me up."

"Why did you need cheering up?"

I shrug. "I'm just in a mood." Or *was* in a mood. Clearly Max's kisses are a much more effective remedy than wine.

He skims his thumb over my bottom lip. "You look beautiful tonight."

"I do?"

Grinning, he tugs me toward the stairs. "Come on. I want to kiss you in front of that bartender."

Present Day

Mom, Granny, and I have been looking at wedding venues, and this is our last stop. I've been tense all morning, but the moment I stepped into the gallery, I remembered Max kissing me for the first time. The memory drained the tension from me like someone turned a release valve in my muscles.

I've always loved this place. William's gallery, the smile on Maggie's face when she works with art, the way the sun shines through the wall of windows at the back and reflects off the stained-glass art hanging from the ceiling. And best of all is the memory of that kiss.

"Hey, girlie. How are you doing?" Maggie asks as I step into the gallery. She's looking especially gorgeous today in a loose-fitting black tank, dark jeans, and strappy sandals.

"I'm good." I force myself to be positive.

Across the street, Max is standing outside the health club,

chatting with a gorgeous, leggy blonde. The old Hanna would have felt twelve kinds of inferior to a girl like that. The old Hanna wouldn't have believed a guy like Max would want a girl like her. Too bad the old Hanna's mind is stuck in the new Hanna's body.

I shift uncomfortably as the girl leans in flirtatiously and presses her hand against Max's chest. I've never had the confidence to be a flirt, but that doesn't mean I don't recognize when someone is putting the moves on my man. Who is she? Some sorority girl he's training? Does he like her?

Max carefully removes her hand from his chest and takes a half-step back.

Next to me, Maggie follows my gaze and snorts. "Don't even worry about it, Han-Han. That boy only has eyes for you."

Mom paces a circle in front of us and frowns. "I'm just not convinced the gallery really gives you enough room for many guests. It would make for a gorgeous, intimate wedding, though, that's for sure."

"I didn't even know Will let people have weddings here," I whisper to Maggie. "I mean, I don't remember if I did know."

"We just started it maybe six months ago," Maggie says. "It works really well. The bride generally comes down the stairs instead of having a traditional aisle, and we have white chairs in storage we can set up here in the lobby for your guests."

"Sounds beautiful."

"It is." Maggie raises a brow. "Have you actually set a date?"

"No, but Mom's pushing me to."

"Nothing pleases that woman more than seeing her daughters marrying good men," Maggie grumbles. "I swear, if she keeps pushing Asher, I'm going to lose my shit."

"So no ring for you yet?" I ask.

Her shoulders tense. "Asher dropped some hints a couple of months back, and I freaked out. I think I scared him, and God knows if he'll ever ask now."

"I'm sure he just wants to make sure you're ready."

She shrugs and waves away the subject. After Maggie's history, I can imagine talk of weddings would panic her a little. I cut my eyes to Max. Only he's not outside anymore, and before I see where he's gone, the bell over the door chimes.

"Hey, Max!" Maggie calls.

From the door, Max grins and runs his eyes over me appreciatively. They're this gorgeous blue that made me weak in the knees back when he didn't notice me, but having them aimed at me like that nearly melts me to the floor.

"Max!" Mom calls, hurrying over to him. "You got my message. I'm so glad you could come over."

The way he just looked at me has my heart pounding triple-time in my chest. Or is that anxiety over what we found on my computer this morning, fear that I've screwed up a good thing?

Max escapes Mom's grasp and then he's spinning me around and grinning at me.

"Pardon me for a moment," he tells Maggie. "I need to kiss my fiancée." He presses his mouth to mine in a kiss that's sweet and tender and sizzles all the way down to my toes. Before I can kiss him back, he's pulling away.

"Hello there," I whisper.

His eyes have gone smoky. He brushes my hair off my shoulders. "I didn't know we were looking at wedding venues."

I settle my hands on his shoulders awkwardly, not sure what else to do with them. After last night, it's funny that I would feel unsure about touching him, but it's not natural to me yet. In my mind, Max is still more *crush* than *fiancé*.

"Mom insisted." I watch him carefully. "Does that make you uncomfortable?"

"We aren't in any rush." He smiles. "Well, *you* aren't. Personally, the sooner I have you sleeping in my bed, the better. Speaking of which, how'd you sleep?" His voice drops, low and husky. He may not have Nate's river-bottom bass, but sweet Jesus, Max does husky well.

"Okay." I force a smile. After he dropped me off at home last night, my conscience kept me up tossing and turning, and my four-thirty alarm came too soon. "What about you?"

He presses a kiss to the crook of my neck. "I would have slept better with you in my arms, but I managed okay." He inhales audibly. "God, you smell so good. What are you wearing?"

That makes me smile. "I think you're smelling sugar cookies and cinnamon muffins. Lizzy and I did a little baking this morning. Making you hungry?"

"Hmm. I'm hungry, all right." He snakes a hand under my shirt and brushes my navel with his thumb, and my mind flashes on the image from the gossip site—me pressed against the side of the building, Nate's hand creeping up my skirt.

I try not to tense. God. This is ridiculous. How can I feel so guilty when I don't even know if I've done anything wrong? *Right. Because there's an innocent explanation to all of this.*

"Mom's having girls' night at her house tonight. She wants to talk wedding plans."

"You should." He pulls his hand from my shirt and smooths the fabric back in place, but his expression is unreadable. "You've been working too hard lately. Not spending enough time with your sisters."

So I'm told. Why didn't he encourage me to spend more time with them back before the accident, when I was alienating Liz? Then again, I've probably been busy with the business and all the exercising. Not to mention a very serious boyfriend and a hottie on the side.

"Want to come with me? Mom wouldn't mind you crashing her dinner."

"I wish I could, but I have a late client again."

A late client. *The same woman as last night?* I bite back the question. I have no right to be suspicious of Max. Quite the opposite.

"The bride can enter from the stairs," Mom's saying. "Guests right there where you two are standing. It would be small but intimate."

"What are you thinking?" Max asks me quietly. "You seem distracted."

I force a smile. We're supposed to be deciding where we're going to exchange vows, and I'm too busy trying to figure out what I've done to pay any attention. "I'm just wondering when you can come by my place so we can pick up where we left off last night?"

"What do *you* think, Max?" Mom asks from the back. "Should

we try to do this in October? Imagine the colorful leaves floating past on the river."

He never takes his eyes from mine. "The sooner the better."

"Great!" She claps her hands gleefully. "Maggie, pull out the calendar for October. Let's set a date!"

Chapter
TEN

"LISTEN." MAX squeezes my hand and tugs me toward the side room and away from Mom and Granny, who are chattering with Maggie over the calendar.

It's done. We set a date. I have six weeks before I marry Max.

This is the room William uses for special collections. The first collection shown in here was of some shockingly intimate portraits of Maggie, but the artist kept it under wraps, so no one knew what he was showing until the opening. Asher bought them all that night, and rumor has it he burned them in a bonfire behind his house.

I don't know what happened between Maggie and the painter, but it sure looked like he'd put her secrets on display. As I scan the walls, now covered with a collection of Maggie's mosaics, I wonder what that would be like—your biggest secrets, your biggest shame on display to the world. Would it be painful, the shock of it? Or would there be an element of relief to know you didn't have to work so hard to hide anymore?

"We need to talk," Max says softly behind me.

I spin around and my stomach pitches at the worry written across his expression. Does he know about Nate? About Sunday night? Does he suspect that another man's been touching me? Kissing me? Sliding his fingers inside me?

The memory sends a shudder through me that's equal parts arousal and fear. I've wanted Max my entire adult life, and I'm terrified I might have ruined my chance.

"What's going on?"

He draws me into his heat and nuzzles his smoothly shaved cheek against my neck. "You smell delicious. It feels so right to have you in my arms again."

"Who's the one with the faulty memory now?" I ask, trying for humor. "I believe you had me in your arms just last night."

He cups my face in his hand. "This is all happening so fast—the wedding date, the venue—"

"Oh my God. You want to call it off?" The words slip from my mouth on a squeak at the same moment my stomach releases from its panicked clench and takes a free fall to the floor.

"No. That's not it." His lips meet mine—firm and sure. It's not a kiss of seduction but one of demand. "I want to marry you. I wouldn't have given you that ring if I hadn't wanted that. But..." His hands fall from my face, and he drags one through his hair. "I know everyone thinks I just proposed last week, but they're wrong."

"What do you mean?"

"I proposed months ago."

Laughter carries from the hallway back to us, and I hear Granny say, "—young, lusty love. Let them have their moment!"

"I don't understand. Then why does everyone think we just got engaged?"

"I gave you the ring, and you..." He turns away, his broad chest lifting on a deep inhale.

Nate. I was going to throw away a life with Max for a fling with some rocker? Was he the reason I told Max I wasn't ready? How stupid could I be?

"I didn't accept," I whisper.

"I don't think you believed I was in love with you." He runs his fingertips lightly over the swirls of yellow glass pieces making up a mosaic interpretation of *Starry Night*.

I'm such an idiot. Because that's something I would do—I'd deny a proposal from a man like Max, a man I've wanted my whole life, just because I didn't believe he really loved me.

"I'm so sorry," I whisper.

He turns back to me and tilts my chin up until he's looking in my eyes. "But I was in love with you, Hanna. And I am. Desperately, hopelessly, helplessly in love."

"Max." I put my hand on his arm. "I was an idiot. I—"

"I told you to keep the ring, that I would wait until you were ready. I was beginning to think you didn't want a future with me. You'd pulled away. We barely spent any time together. We were just in this hellish limbo while I waited for you to decide."

"I'm so sorry," I repeat.

"Don't be. Because then I got to the hospital and you were wearing the ring. You were confused and beat up and it was terrifying, but every time I saw that ring on your finger, I believed everything was going to be okay. It had to be."

"Sounds like I'd finally come to my senses." But what damage had I done in the weeks between?

"You needed to know. No one else does. We kept it quiet. I wanted the decision to be yours. All that matters is that you decided to put on the ring. And when I saw you in that hospital bed, my ring on your finger..." He shakes his head. Swallows. "God, it's such a cliché, but you've truly made me the happiest man in the world. You owe me no apologies."

"What I did hurt you." I glance over my shoulder to make sure our private conversation stays that way. "I owe you every apology for that." And maybe more than an apology. Maybe an explanation. Maybe the truth.

He draws me against him and crushes me to his chest, and I breathe him in and swallow back my tears. I could tell him. Maybe I should, but the idea of losing this...

I look up at him. "When *did* you propose?" I ask quietly.

"Three months ago."

"I brought the booze," Granny says when my mom leaves her dining room to retrieve dessert. She pulls a flask from her skirt, unscrews the cap, and takes a gulp before passing it to me.

I grin and take a swig myself before passing it on to Lizzy.

"Oh, Hanna, I've been dying to do something about this." She grabs at the air around my head, flicking away invisible pieces of God-knows-what.

"Granny, what are you *doing*?" Liz asks.

"Apparently Hanna neglected to keep her aura clean while in the hospital," Maggie grouses as she takes her turn with the flask.

"No, it's been like this for months." Granny shudders, flicking away more invisible aura ugliness. "Come to my office for a thorough cleansing. No bride should go into her wedding day with so much darkness in her aura."

"I'll think about it," I lie.

I have the world's coolest grandmother—as evidenced by the fact that she cashed in one of her investments to buy each of her granddaughters her own muscle car a couple of years back. But she's also the world's kookiest grandmother. I squirm under her assessing gaze, relaxing only when she shifts it to Maggie.

"Yours looks better than it has since you were fourteen," Granny tells Maggie. "I told your mother she shouldn't stop you from shacking up with that rocker. Best thing that ever happened to you."

Maggie blushes—a rare sight. "Thanks. I think so too." Then Mom's coming back into the room, and Maggie has to hide the flask under the table.

"Where is the Sexy Beast anyway, Maggie?" Granny asks, using Asher's music-world nickname.

"He has a concert in Chicago tonight," Maggie says. "It's sweet of you to ask."

Lizzy snorts. "Granny's only asking because she wants her eye candy back."

Granny winks. "Damn straight."

"Nanci!" Mom protests.

Granny shrugs. "What? I might be old but my eyes work just fine, thank you very much. And your daughters are doing a mighty fine job of giving me nice views as I go into old age."

"Well, it doesn't bother me at all if you want to check out my man," Maggie says. "But he and Nate are touring together for the next week and a half, so you'll have to wait."

"Will he be home a week from Saturday?" Mom asks. "I'm throwing a casual engagement party for your sister."

Casual. I'm sure. Mom doesn't know the meaning of the word. Case in point, the crystal goblet holding my water.

"When he comes back into town, he'll have Nate with him. They're trying to get a project finished up by the end of the month, so he'll be busy, but I'm sure he can get away for a couple of hours."

Lizzy and I exchange a look, and I force myself to relax as Lizzy leans across the table toward Maggie, an interrogator going in for the kill. "So Nate's coming back to town? Will he be staying at your house?"

Maggie rolls her eyes. "I think it's in Nate's best interest that I not tell you where he's sleeping, Liz. No offense."

"They'll probably have to work late into the night though, huh?" Liz asks.

Laughter bursts from Maggie's lips. "You're pathetic. If the guys emerge from their music-making cave long enough to have a beer, I promise to invite you over."

Lizzy squeaks, and I elbow her under the table. "Calm down," I say between my teeth.

"Thanks for dinner, Mom." She pushes her plate away and looks at me pointedly. "Hanna, were you going to come back to the bakery with me tonight? To work on the calla lilies for Saturday's wedding cake?"

"Sure." I'm halfway through the three dozen gum-paste lilies I need to decorate Saturday's monstrosity of a cake order.

"I'll see you later," Maggie calls.

As we head out the front door, I can hear Mom talking. "You could learn a thing or two from Hanna, Maggie. Instead of giving it up to Max the first chance she got, she's waiting until marriage.

Maybe if you weren't living with Asher, you'd be wearing his ring by now. You know what they say about the cow and the milk."

I turn to Lizzy, wide-eyed, and she throws a hand over her mouth. I open the door just as Maggie says, "Mom, if you think sex is like milk, you're doing it wrong."

Lizzy and I are laughing by the time we climb into Lizzy's car, and I have to lean my head back against the seat and catch my breath.

"Here's the plan," Lizzy says when we're on the road and headed to the bakery. "We're going over there when Nate comes back into town. You'll corner him. Get some answers."

The smile falls from my face. "What if I don't want the answers?" I whisper. "I mean, I do. Of course I do. But I'm scared, Liz."

She pulls into a spot in front of the building and puts the car in park before reaching over to squeeze my hand. "You could just wait and see if your memories come back."

"They're starting to. I remember more every day, but it's all stuff from fall semester and the beginning of my relationship with Max. None of my memories are answering my questions yet."

We go inside the bakery and head to the back, working together to pull out supplies for Saturday's calla lily explosion.

"Today, Max told me something." I run my fingers along the prepared flowers, searching for imperfections. "He didn't propose right before my accident like everyone assumed."

Lizzy frowns. "Then where'd the ring come from?"

"He proposed before that. A *long time* before that. And I told him I wasn't ready."

She covers her lips with her fingers and studies me. "You've always wanted Max."

"I know."

"When did he propose?"

"Three months ago." I drop the flower I was inspecting and walk to the back door and push it open. I can't breathe. I need fresh air. "I didn't give him an answer and held on to the ring all this time."

"Three months ago?" She arches a brow. "As in, *after* you met a sexy rocker?"

"That's what I'm afraid of," I say.

"I think we're still missing something," she says.

"What do you mean?"

"That night you came home from the hospital and Nate climbed in bed with you in the middle of the night... Did you lock the door?"

"I did. I'm sure of it."

"So you gave him a key." She nods. "That says something about your relationship, I think."

"Why would I give him a key?" Panic starts that slow-clawing climb in my chest. "Didn't you say he'd never been to town?"

She shrugs. "Maybe you knew he'd be coming."

"And I gave him a key when *Max* already has one? Really? I mean, I was obviously being reckless, but that seems a little over the top."

"So you think he broke in?"

"I don't know," I whisper. "But I know I locked the door."

"What if he had a key for a different reason?" Liz asks.

"I'm not following."

"What if he has a key to your apartment because he owns the building? What if *Nate* is your silent partner?"

"Fuck," I whisper.

"Think about the timeline. You go to Asher's concert and meet Nate either shortly before or shortly after Max proposes, and within a couple of weeks, someone's buying this vacant building downtown and setting it up to be your bakery and apartment. Maybe you screwed around with Nate because you were feeling insecure and then he offered you your dream on a platter right before Max proposed."

"Why would Nate buy a bakery for a woman he just met? And if I was committed to Max, why would I let him?"

"Girl, your life has gotten better than my daytime soaps. *Days of Our Lives* cannot compete with this shit."

"Maybe I wasn't choosing Nate over Max. Maybe I was choosing my business over Max. I mean, what if Nate does own it and he was going to sell it or something if I married Max?"

"That would be pretty dickish."

"Yes, but he's a spoiled rock star. Of course he'd be a dick about getting his way, right?"

She frowns. "That's one big insult to his personality wrapped up in a clichéd assumption."

"Even if there were no strings attached to our agreement, that's gotta be awkward, right? What if Max marries me and finds out I'm in business with the guy I was once cheating on him with?" I gasp and throw my hand over my mouth. "Liz, Max and I are planning on living upstairs after we get married!"

"Shit," she breathes. "You need to find out if Nate's the silent partner."

I nod. "And I need to find out before the wedding."

Chapter
ELEVEN

"Iт's so screwed up," Drew says. "The whole town hates her and thinks she's this total slut, but nobody really cares that it takes two, you know?" She scoops the cookies off the tray and slides them onto a cooling rack. "Can you imagine if we made all the cheating *men* walk around with a red A on their chests? No one would be ashamed. They'd just wear it all proud. Probably be embarrassed if they didn't have one. I swear. I hate the world sometimes."

I bite back my laughter. Drew's junior honors English class is American Literature, and she has to finish *The Scarlet Letter* before school starts on Monday. Just yesterday, she was groaning about having to read "this stupid old book," and now she's so into it she can hardly stop talking about it.

"I've made my last latte," Lizzy says, pushing into the kitchen. "I'm tapping out. Drew. You're up."

Drew groans but otherwise doesn't protest before going to man the front of the store.

"Thank God," Liz says when Drew's safely on the other side of the kitchen door. "I had to get her away from you before you started getting a complex and embroidering an A on all your clothes."

I wrinkle my nose. "I didn't even think of that, but thanks. Thanks a lot."

"So did you make an appointment with the lawyer to find out about the silent partner?"

I nod. "I'm going in next week."

"Good. Want me to go with you?"

I bite my lip and nod. "Is that pathetic?"

She rolls her eyes. "No. I'm, like, your assistant manager or some shit. What affects your business affects me."

"Thank you so much. The lawyer's in Indianapolis, and I'm not supposed to be driving."

"And you're a scaredy cat."

"True fact." I grab a hot pad and swat her with it before opening the oven.

The chocolate chip scones smell so delicious my mouth literally waters as I pull them out of the oven. I've been trying to be good about my eating. I haven't even been home from the hospital a week, and I've already gained weight. Dr. Perkins doesn't want me getting on the scale, but I don't need a scale when it's getting harder to button my jeans.

"Do it," Lizzy says behind me. She grabs one off the tray and breaks a corner off to pop it in her mouth. Her eyes float closed and she moans. "Jesus Christ, Hanna. I don't need a man. I just need your baked goods. *All* of your baked goods." She grabs my forearm and squeezes. "Promise me you'll never cut me off."

I giggle and break a piece off her scone. The butter and flour practically melt on my tongue. "God, I'm good."

"Are you sure you want to be eating that?" someone asks at the door.

Lizzy and I turn to find my mother walking into my kitchen with her old critical eyes on my baked goods. I'm not used to my mom looking at me with approval. She's terrified of fat, extra weight, and clothing sizes in the double digits. My inability to keep my weight down was always a point of anxiety for her. And I always felt like a failure. Until I woke up in the hospital with my new body. Then all that disappointment was gone from her eyes.

It's back now as she eyes the half-eaten scone in Lizzy's hand.

"She's sure," Lizzy says. "It's delicious, and she hasn't stopped working all day to eat lunch."

I think about it and realize she's right. I had some plain oatmeal for breakfast around five, but I haven't had anything since. No wonder I'm famished.

Mom lifts a brown paper bag and beams. "That's why I brought you a healthy lunch."

I have to bite back a groan. My old self hated the crap she used to feed me. Leafy greens without dressing, carrots, and way more chicken breast than any reasonable human would want to consume. Hell, the boob-loving men of the world should probably thank her. It was probably all those hormone-filled chicken breasts that gave me boobs by age thirteen.

"What did you bring?" Liz asks. "Some weeds and sticks for her to nibble on?"

"Elizabeth," Mom scolds. "We can't all have your metabolism. And that's going to catch up with you someday."

Lizzy glares defiantly and takes another big bite of her scone.

"Stop trying to make me out to be the bad guy here," Mom objects. "I'm just helping Hanna with something she decided was important to her *months* ago."

My size has always been important to me. Because she taught me to believe it was. But three months ago it must have become so important that I took measures I'd never stooped to before. Last night I found diet pills in the back of my cabinet. Add those to the starvation and unhealthy amounts of exercise. And so much of it cloaked in secrecy that it sickens me to think about it.

But Mom doesn't know about Dr. Perkins. She doesn't know I was making myself sick.

There's no reason to make her worry, though, so I paste on a smile and say, "What's for lunch?"

Mom smiles approvingly. "Chopped grilled chicken, greens, and a tiny sliver of avocado in a low-carb, whole-grain wrap." She hands the bag over, and I dig out her homemade lunch. "Eat, and then we have an appointment at Cleanstein's."

I pause with the wrap halfway to my mouth. "At the wedding dress shop?"

"Of course. You're getting married in five weeks. We're going to have to buy off the rack as is. We need to start shopping last week."

I try to swallow around the tightness in my throat. Is no one going to ask if I *want* to be planning my wedding? If I *want* to rush my engagement?

Mom sniffs, and I realize there are tears in her eyes. "After Maggie's canceled wedding and Krystal's disaster of a ceremony, you can imagine how excited I am about yours." She squeezes my hand. "There's just something so special about Max."

"Speak of the devil," Liz mutters as Max pushes through the door into the kitchen.

My heart stumbles in my chest at the sight of him. He's got a light stubble going on today, and he's still disheveled from his run.

"Oh, hello, Max!" my mom croons. God, she loves him so much.

"How are New Hope's three most beautiful women?" he asks with a wink.

"We're peachy," Liz says. "How's New Hope's biggest suck-up?"

Max draws me into a hug and presses a kiss to my forehead. "Does your sister hate me?" he asks loud enough for her to hear.

"No. She's just cranky that Mom didn't bring her lunch."

Lizzy snorts at the same moment my mom says, "Oh, I'm so sorry, Liz! I won't forget you next time!"

"How are you?" I ask Max. We've barely seen each other the last few days. He almost always trains late at the club, and I get horrible headaches if I don't get enough rest, so I've been going to bed early. I haven't found the courage to ask him to sleep with me—in the literal or figurative sense of the phrase.

"I'm good," he says. "What are you up to this afternoon? Can I steal you away for a while? I miss my girl." He ducks his head and steals a bite of my wrap, and because there's something very twisted and wrong with me, I actually find the movement of his jaw as he chews sexy as all hell. Then again, it's Max, and everything he does is sexy.

"No horning in on our plans this afternoon," Mom says. "We are going wedding dress shopping."

Max's eyes light up and he looks at me like I've just given him some amazing gift. "Yeah?"

I'm gonna burn in hell for hurting this sweet, sweet man. "Yeah," I say, though I hadn't even decided until that moment that I was going to let my mom talk me into it.

Max grins. "Well, I guess I can sacrifice an afternoon with you if that's the reason behind it."

"There are plenty of plans you can join us for," Mom assures him. "I have appointments with three caterers lined up for next week."

"Wow, Mom," Liz says. "Whose wedding is this anyway?"

"This is really happening, isn't it?" Max asks, and there's so much joy in his eyes that I'm reminded of the day at the gallery when he told me about my initial lack of response to his proposal. *"I was beginning to think you didn't want a future with me."*

He's had enough limbo, hasn't he? Can I really ask for him to endure more? And if Max is the man I want and he wants me, what's the harm in getting married quickly?

"Oh, Max, you sweet thing," Mom says, "of course this is happening."

"That is *the one*," Mom declares an hour into dress shopping.

I would have hated every minute of this at my old size. Putting on these dresses and modeling them for my critical mother—it would have pretty much been my own personal hell.

But at this size, it's not so bad. The attendant brings in dress after dress, seemingly unconcerned about my own personal taste and style, and my mom dotes on me in every one. Even in the dresses she doesn't like, she squeaks when I walk out of the dressing room.

And the way she's looking at me in this one makes the little girl in me—the one desperate for her approval—so gleefully happy. I know this will be the dress we buy, regardless of how I feel about the style.

"Take your hair down," Mom says. She comes up behind me and releases my barrette to let my heavy, dark hair fall past my shoulders. "Get her a veil," she calls to the attendant.

The attendant rushes over with a veil in the same super-soft fabric featured on the dress and slides it into my hair.

"It's perfect, isn't it, sweetheart?"

When she turns me to face the big three-panel mirror, I can't reply. I look like...a bride.

"It's perfect," Mom says for me. "We're getting this one. No question."

It's not something I would have picked. It's fitted all the way down through the hips and is covered with twinkling rhinestones. It's one of those dresses I would love for someone else, but it's not really for me. I always pictured myself getting married in something softer. Simpler.

"We're in a tight timeline," Mom says. "What kind of discount can you give me if we buy off the rack?"

The attendant and Mom haggle over price as I stare at my reflection. It's just a dress. It doesn't really matter if it's my dream dress. All that matters is the guy. All that matters is Max.

February—Six Months Before Accident

"Would you get out from in front of that mirror?" Lizzy calls from the front room of our rental. "You look freaking gorgeous, and Max is going to think so too."

I blink at my reflection, as if moistening my eyes could make me see what Lizzy sees, but it's still me standing here. Me. Chubby. Plain. Trying too hard.

I chose black pants and a black scoop-neck sweater for tonight. No frills to distract from the two features of my outfit I do feel confident about: my cleavage and my sexy red heels.

I grab the curling iron and add a couple of fresh ringlets to hair. Max likes my hair. I said something about cutting it off last week, and he looked horrified. *"You have great hair. Why would you cut something so beautiful?"*

The ringing of the doorbell pulls me away from the mirror, and by the time I reach the front room, Max is already here, a bunch of red roses in his hands.

Lizzy shakes her head. "I fucking hate this holiday."

"I told you Sam wanted to take you out tonight," Max tells her.

Liz snorts. "Sam wanted to *fuck* me tonight. Pardon me for holding out for something more romantic than a low-budget porno on Valentine's Day."

Max laughs. "He would have given you all the romance you could handle."

"He asked if I was open to a threesome," Lizzy growls.

I bite back a smile. The relationship between Liz and Sam is a bit of a love-hate situation, and he likes to razz her by asking her for sexual favors.

"You know he really likes you," Max says. "He's just doesn't think you'd take him seriously."

Liz shakes her head and turns to me with a mischievous smile. "I'm out of here. You two have a nice night."

Then she leaves, and Max and I are left alone for the Valentine's Day dinner I cooked for him. I liked the idea of being here and drinking too much wine. Maybe then I could get over myself enough to let him touch me. The high-school-caliber groping we have going on is nice, but I know Max is ready for more.

I take the flowers into the kitchen, where I've already set the small table for our dinner.

"It smells amazing in here," he says. "What are we having?"

"Filet mignon with green beans and a fresh French baguette and then chocolate lava cake for dessert." I fill a vase with water and arrange the roses in it before setting it on the table. When I turn around, Max is right there, his face inches from mine.

"Happy Valentine's Day," he whispers. He lowers his mouth to mine in a kiss so sweet my nerves fizzle away. And maybe it's how good he smells or the fact that I already had a big glass of wine before he got here. Or maybe it's because I'm standing and don't feel as self-conscious about my body like this. But when his hands find the hem of my sweater and slide under, I don't stop him.

He breaks the kiss and leans his forehead against mine, his eyes closed and lips parted a fraction of an inch as he cups my breast in his hand and grazes his thumb over my nipple. The contact makes my knees weak and I have to curl my hands into the thick muscle of his shoulders to keep myself upright.

"So we have the place to ourselves tonight?" he whispers.

Something thick lodges in my throat at his question and nerves flare back to life in my belly. "Yeah."

"Do you want to have dinner first or can I give you your present?"

"I thought the flowers were my present."

He grins and points to a gift bag sitting by the door. "I got you something else too."

"You really didn't have to."

He retrieves the bag and watches me carefully as I open it.

"Oh." It's pretty much the last thing I'd want him to buy me.

"Do you like it?"

"I..." I force a smile but it hurts when I want to die of mortification. "It's beautiful. Thank you." And it is. The silky gold material of the lingerie slip is rose-petal soft in my hands and beautiful against my skin.

"I know you're not ready yet. I don't want you to think I'm pushing you. But I saw it and I thought of you. You'd look gorgeous in it."

"Thank you," I repeat, dropping it back into the bag. I have to turn away from him. I can't let him know how horrified I am by the idea of him seeing me in that slip. I don't want him to see the parts of me that would be on display in it or to know how un-sexy a girl like me looks in lingerie.

I go back to the kitchen and busy myself with the steaks.

"Did I do something wrong?" he asks behind me. "Was that too much too soon or...?"

"No," I assure him. "You're wonderful. This is perfect." But the awkward silence as I get our meals on the table speaks volumes to how not-perfect this night is shaping up to be.

"Want me to pour some wine?" he asks as I take our plates to the table.

My shoulders drop in relief. Wine is just the Band-Aid we need here. "That would be wonderful."

He pours us each a full glass and we sit and stare awkwardly at our food. "I'm sorry about the lingerie. It's probably too soon for that."

Shit. I've ruined this. I keep reminding myself that I can't have it both ways. I can't be with Max in every way I want to *and* keep hiding my body from him. "I'm kind of…insecure," I blurt.

Looking up from his plate, he softens. "I noticed." He isn't cruel about it. It isn't an accusation—more of a sympathetic understanding.

"I saw the slip and instantly thought about how much I didn't want you to see me in it." God, that's terrible to admit.

"Hanna…" He exhales heavily. "I don't know what to say. I wouldn't have bought it for you if I didn't want to see you wear it."

"I'm not like the girls you usually date."

"Thank God." He grins. "You're you. And I happen to like that." His phone buzzes and he pulls it from his pocket. "Sorry," he says as he slides his finger over the screen and reads. "Crap."

"What is it?"

"Meredith thinks she's going into pre-term labor. She wants me to take her to the hospital."

"Meredith? The one who bought sperm to get pregnant and let everyone think it was William Bailey's baby?"

He taps something on his phone before sliding it back into his pocket. I wait for him to respond, but his mind is somewhere else already. "I'm sorry. She doesn't have anyone else to take her." He stands, and I'm so shocked I can only gape at him. "I'll make it up to you, okay?"

I shake my head as if the motion can send my confusion away. What is happening? Is my boyfriend seriously going to spend Valentine's Day with some pregnant bitch who tried to steal my best friend's boyfriend?

By the time I can gather my wits to follow him to the door, he's already in his coat and pulling open the door.

"It's Valentine's Day," I whisper.

He drags a hand through his hair, tousling it in the way that makes him go from handsome to devilishly irresistible. "She doesn't have anyone."

"What about her friends? I happen to remember her having a lot of those back when she was letting everyone think William was some jerk who got her knocked up."

His jaw hardens. "I know Cally's your friend, but Meredith is mine. You're going to have to deal with that."

He pushes out the door and pulls it shut behind him, and I'm left alone with a romantic dinner complete with wine, roses, and lingerie. Alone while he runs to rescue the gorgeous blonde.

Chapter
TWELVE

"IT's NICE to see you again, Miss Thompson," the lawyer says as Lizzy and I settle into chairs in her comfortable Indianapolis office. "And it's nice to meet your sister. What can I do for you today?"

"We're kind of wondering who the silent partner is," Liz says. She points her thumb at me. "This one has amnesia and doesn't remember whether or not you told her."

Her eyes go wide. "Amnesia! That's horrible. I'm so sorry. What happened?"

"I'm a klutz and fell down the stairs."

"Goodness. Do they think your memory will come back?"

"The doctor said it will, but like Swiss cheese," I explain. "And so far that's been true. Lots of holes, including the details of my agreement with my silent partner."

"Well, to answer your sister's first question, the agreement was under the condition of my client's anonymity, so if you knew who was behind it, that information certainly didn't come from me." She stands and hands me a thick folder across the desk. "I'm sure you have this in your files somewhere, but those are copies with the details of our agreement. You may keep them if you like."

I open the file and flip through the first few pages, but my impatient twin cuts to the chase. "What's going to happen to the bakery when she gets married?"

She lifts a brow. "I'm not sure what you mean."

I shift awkwardly. "What my sister is trying to say is, not knowing who the silent partner is, I'm not sure if it would be okay for my husband and me to live in the apartment over the bakery. Or if my...partner would have an issue with that."

She frowns. "I'd be happy to check with my client, but I can't imagine he would object. Those living quarters didn't come with any stipulations that I recall."

Lizzy and I exchange a look, and Liz says, "You really can't tell us? Not even a hint?"

The lawyer looks unimpressed with my sister's adorable persistence. "Not even a hint, Miss Thompson. That's the definition of *anonymous*."

I dreamed about Nate Crane last night. We were swimming in Asher's pool and he stripped my swimsuit off my breasts and took my nipples into his mouth. I wrapped my legs around his waist and realized he was nude and his dick was cradled right between my legs.

"We can't have sex," I said in the dream. "I'm marrying Max."

"No you're not."

He slid the ring off my finger and threw it into the deep end of the water. Only we weren't in the pool anymore. We were in the river. The ring glinted against the moonlight before the dark water sucked it under, and I knew I'd never see it again. I just shrugged, and Nate slid his hand between my legs. Then we were in Max's steam room. I was sitting on the high bench just like I had the night I was there with Max, only it was Nate with me. Nate's face buried between my legs. Nate's fingers toying with my nipples.

And when Max walked into the room and called my name through the steam, I laughed. "*This is what you wanted*," I said, grabbing a fistful of Nate's hair and holding him against me. "*You wanted me to find someone else, and I did. Now go fuck a blonde."*

I woke up confused, horny, guilty, and depressed. Did it mean something, or is my brain just screwed up from how crazy everything's been the last few weeks?

I've been home from the hospital for two weeks and I feel like I never see Max. He works late almost every night, and when he does come over, he doesn't stay long. And we've never had sex. I know he's turned on by me—it's evident—but it's almost like he's perfectly satisfied to stop things with a little groping.

In the meantime, wedding planning is going full speed ahead. I ended up having a meeting at the bakery during our caterer appointments last week, so Mom went with Max and they picked a caterer without me. I was relieved not to have to mess with it. Shouldn't I be more excited about my wedding?

From the edge of Mom's back deck, I scan the crowd gathered for my engagement party and try to push my anxiety to the side.

In just two weeks, Mom pulled together a party to rival the weddings of most girls in this town. I didn't give her any input on the event, but then again, she didn't ask for any. Not too different than my wedding, now that I think of it.

Nix Reid, my doctor and apparently friend, sidles up to me and puts her hand on my arm. "You look stressed. Are you okay?"

I force a smile. "I'm great. Turned out beautifully, didn't it?"

The evening is warm but not too warm to mingle out on the lawn. Servers circulate with hors d'oeuvres, and Mom hired a bartender to serve drinks from a makeshift bar on the deck.

On the lawn, a small band is playing in front of the temporary floor put down so our guests can dance under the stars. It's beautiful and perfect and terrifying.

"It's a lovely party." She smooths her hair and shifts awkwardly. She doesn't seem like a woman who's comfortable in dress clothes. "How are you feeling?"

"I'm doing great, really." I pause for a breath. "Do you have any guess as to when my other memories might come back?"

Nix looks around. "This is what you want to talk about right now?" She puts her hand on my shoulder and smiles. "Relax. Stressing about your memory isn't going to help anything."

"It's just weird," I say. "I'm getting these pieces back, but the last few months are still completely missing. Like they never happened." And the last few months are the memories I want the most.

"Memory recovery isn't an exact science. It's different for everyone, but it does usually happen chronologically—not always, but for the most part. Just because you don't have any memories from the last few months doesn't mean you won't."

"There's so much I still don't know. And the day of the accident? The day I fell down the stairs?" *The day I put on Max's ring.* "I want that back. I want it all back."

"Listen," she says. "The worse the head trauma, the less likely you are to remember the events leading up to it. You need to make peace with the possibility that you might never recover your memories of the accident or the days prior."

Including the day I chose Max. "This sucks."

She whispers, "I know, but let it go. For tonight at least, okay? Try to enjoy your party. I'll see you in my office next week."

"Where's the couple of honor?" the bandleader asks in the mic. "Because I understand this is their song." The guitar player starts into the first notes of Jason Mraz's "I Won't Give Up."

Suddenly, Max is next to me, taking my hand and leading me to the dance floor.

"This is our song?" I ask as I slip my arms around his neck.

"I gave you the ring three months ago, remember?"

Something squeezes in my chest as the man sings the line about giving his love the space she needs to navigate. Is that what Max did for me? Gave me the space I needed to figure this out? I want to remember.

"You look drop-dead gorgeous tonight," he murmurs against my ear.

I'm wearing a red dress, a bold, daring color that draws attention to my legs and my curves. Not just any red dress. It's Lizzy's. The one she wore to the winter gallery opening. Now I remember the night I caught Max checking her out and felt twelve kinds of depressed about it…until he kissed me silly.

"You know what I think would be even more gorgeous than

you in that dress?"

"What's that?" I ask.

"You out of that dress. In my bed."

A delicious chill runs over my skin, but he says stuff like that and then...nothing.

He pulls me even closer and I can feel that hard length of him through his dress pants. "That's all I've been able to think about since I had to leave you last night—undressing you and taking you to my bed, keeping you there all weekend."

"I think I'd like that." I've not pushed the issue of our lack of intimacy. My head's too busy spinning with what I have and haven't done, but I'm ready to put a stop to that hesitancy. I'm marrying this man, and none of my memories of making love to him have returned yet. I want to know what that's like. I want the *reassurance* of him making love to me.

He groans. "I'd make damn sure you liked it."

"Don't make promises you don't intend to keep."

His hands tighten on me, pulling me closer. "Don't tempt me. We've made it this far. We can hold out for a few more weeks, don't you think?"

I stop moving. Right there in the middle of the dance floor, my shoes might as well be filled with lead. "What?"

"Don't get me wrong," he says quietly. "I want you. You don't need to question that. I want you like I've never wanted anyone." He presses his nose to my hair and inhales deeply. "But there's something kind of special about waiting, about the anticipation of it. And I'm sorry if it's not politically correct, but I fucking love that I'm going to be your first and only."

I push back half a step so I can look into his eyes. "Are you saying we've never...?"

Confusion flashes in his eyes. Then he drags a hand over his face. "God, it never occurred to me that I needed to tell you, but how would you know if you can't remember?"

"Know what?" I need to hear him say it.

He smiles, as if he's about to tell me some delightful surprise. "You're a virgin," he whispers. "You wanted to wait for marriage." He pulls me back against him, and I press my hot cheek against his chest and squeeze my eyes shut.

"*You're a virgin.*" But what he means is that I haven't slept with *him*. Did I sleep with Nate?

The song ends, and he tips my chin up to look in my eyes. "Are you okay?"

I don't trust myself to talk, so I nod toward the bar.

We walk hand in hand. Every brush of his thumb skimming over my knuckles digs a guilty dagger into my heart. Every day it becomes clearer to me that I have secrets I have to share with Max before we can get married, but it never occurred to me I might have to tell him I gave my virginity to someone else.

Lizzy's standing in front of the bar in a long, strapless black dress, tapping her foot to the beat. She takes in our joined hands and grins. "You two look nice out there."

Max presses a kiss to the back of my hand and winks at me. "This beauty can make anyone look good."

Lizzy's jaw goes slack and she flashes me a look as if to say, "How could you *doubt* a future with this guy?" Or maybe it's more, "You are such a bitch." As her twin, I'm excellent at reading her, but those are pretty similar looks.

"What can I get you?" the bartender asks.

Max stuffs a five in the tip jar. "A draft beer for me and a glass of Riesling for my girl." The bartender hands us our glasses, and Max presses a kiss to my bare shoulder. "I need to talk to William about our plans for his bachelor party. Sam made plans at this strip club in Indy and Will isn't having it. Apparently, I'm supposed to be the mediator."

"Mediate away." I force a smile. "I'm not going anywhere."

"I love you," he whispers.

I wait until he's gone before I turn to Liz and drag her into Mom's house and all the way upstairs to our old bedroom.

"What's going on?" she asks as I shut the door.

"Max said I'm a virgin."

Her eyes go big and her jaw drops.

"He said I wanted to wait until we got married to have sex."

"Since…when?"

I let out a long breath and study the ceiling. This is all so weird.

Some days it doesn't even feel like I missed a year of my life. It feels like I was dropped into someone else's.

"I just assumed you two had had sex."

"That makes two of us."

"You and Mom have gotten closer lately," she says. "Maybe she brought you over to the devout side?"

"I'm not buying that."

"Yeah. Me neither. But hey, at least that means you didn't have sex with Nate Crane either, right?"

"But what if I did?" I whisper.

"Oh." She plops down on the bed. "That would be really bad, wouldn't it? Max thinking you're a virgin and you actually already gave that up to someone else?"

"I have to tell Max what I know."

"Why?"

"Lizzy, I'm marrying him."

"Exactly."

"I need to be honest. I need him to know what I've done."

"If you had your memories, I might agree, but the truth is, until they come back, you don't know the whole story. The only thing you're going to accomplish by telling Max is hurting him."

"So you're saying I shouldn't tell the man I'm marrying that I was seeing someone else? Possibly *sleeping* with someone else? I shouldn't explain to him why I wouldn't wear his ring all those months?"

"That's exactly what I'm saying."

"My memories are starting to come back."

"More since last time?"

I nod. "It's weird, you know. I get these snippets, and a lot of them are insignificant. I remember jogging with Max in the mornings. I remember going into his gym and asking him to train me. I remember the first time he kissed me at the winter gallery opening."

"Anything about Nate?"

I shake my head. "And nothing to make me think I would have had a reason to cheat on Max." Except for my profound insecurity. What if I never got over that feeling that I wasn't good enough for Max? What if those feelings made me do something really stupid? And what about Valentine's Day, when he left me alone to take care of Meredith? Is that just the price of dating a good guy? Or was something going on there?

She taps her knee thoughtfully. "None of this makes sense. Cheating? That's just not in character for you. Maybe you didn't realize things with Max were going anywhere. Maybe you didn't think he was serious about you."

"You forget that he proposed *three months* ago."

"Crap. That's right."

"Girls!" Mom calls from downstairs. "What are you doing up there? Come down to the party!"

"Coming!" I call back.

Lizzy's staring at me. "Are you sure you're okay with this? Not all the memory loss and bad crap, but marrying Max? Is this what you want?"

"Of course." But in that moment, with everyone waiting downstairs to congratulate me and ask questions about how many babies we plan to have, I'm not sure if this is really what I want or what I *should* want.

Chapter
THIRTEEN

Max props his bare feet on my coffee table and sips a beer. I had no idea a man's bare feet could be so damn sexy.

The engagement party couldn't have gone any better, but I'm glad it's over. As soon as we got back to my apartment, all my fears and insecurities faded away. Because Max makes me feel good.

"I hear you picked out a dress last week," Max says.

"I'm not sure if *I* picked it out or my mom did, but that's more or less true."

He frowns. "Do you like it?"

"It's beautiful, and hopefully *you* will like it."

I take the beer from his hands and set it on the end table before straddling him. I'm still in the red dress, in no hurry to put an end to the way his eyes roam over me while I'm wearing it.

I sink onto his lap, my knees on either side of his hips. His gaze floats down to the dress's low neckline and he swallows.

"I've missed you this last week." I rub my fingers over the stubble of his jaw. "Are you working a lot more than usual or is this normal?"

He shrugs. "Money's a little tight and I had to let a couple of part-timers go. Summer's always slow. It'll pick up when the semester starts and the Sinclair students decide they want to work out in something nicer than the dungeon that the college tries to pass off as a gym."

"Hmm. Well, we'll have to figure out how I can see you more."

"When your doctor says it's okay, we'll run together again. That was always *us* time."

I arch a brow. "No offense to your very healthy-sounding plans, but I had a different kind of exercise in mind."

His eyes darken, his pupils dilating, and I slip the dress's thin straps from my shoulders.

He slides his hands under the soft cotton and cups my ass. "Hanna?"

"Mmm?" My eyes float closed as his fingers massage into tight muscles.

"What happened to your underwear?"

I look up at him through my lashes. "I took them off when I got home. Seemed like they might just be in the way."

I kiss the corner of his mouth, the stubble at the edge of his jaw, and open my mouth against his neck. He yanks my hips forward and lifts his in one liquid movement, pressing my exposed sex to the hard denim of his jeans.

"You know the worst thing about our night in the steam room?"

I pull back. "I didn't know there was a worst thing."

"Oh, there was something." He traces my bottom lip with his thumb. "I couldn't see you. I want to see you."

He wraps his arms around me and stands. I squeak and wrap my legs around him, locking my ankles behind his back to hold on.

He carries me to the bedroom, lowers me to the bed, and clicks on the light on the bedside table.

Slowly, he trails his gaze over me, from my red-painted toenails to my thighs. I lift off the bed as he grips the hem of the dress and pulls it off over my head. His eyes are hot when they return to mine. Hot and needy. It takes my breath.

He pulls off his shirt and climbs next to me in his jeans. I wish he'd get naked, but his hands are on me before I can ask, his fingers following the path his eyes just took—from my toes, up my calves, to my thighs. He hesitates between my legs and skims a finger right over my center before resuming his northward journey over my navel and to my breasts.

I'm already wet and aching and breathing heavily, and he hasn't done anything but skim his fingers over me.

"Tell me what you like."

What I *like*? Who would know that better than him? "I just—"

His phone beeps and buzzes from his pocket. "Sorry." He digs it out and tosses it on the floor without looking at it. "You were saying?"

I shrug, suddenly self-conscious. "You. That's what I like. Just you."

He groans and lowers his mouth to mine, one leg nestled between my thighs.

His phone beeps and buzzes again, clattering against the floor.

"You should check that," I say against his lips.

He exhales heavily and climbs off me to retrieve it, but when he looks at the screen, something in his face changes. "I'm so sorry. I'm going to have to go." He taps the screen and shoves the phone back into his pocket. When he looks at me again, he rakes his gaze over me and shakes his head. "I don't want to, but I have to."

I push onto my elbows and frown. "What's wrong? Who was that?"

"It's a friend." He grabs his shirt off the floor and tugs it on over his head. "I'll fill you in on the details later, but I have to go help her out."

Her? My hands shake as I pull my dress back on and follow him to the door. He shoves his feet into his shoes, and my stomach twists. My voice is weak when I ask, "Who?"

I can tell by the way he stiffens that I'm not going to like the answer. "Meredith."

The name hits me like a punch in the gut. *Meredith.* My mind conjures the images of him leaving on Valentine's Day. His sweet attention completely diverted the moment she texted. The way he hurried out the door when she needed him. And now, on the night of our fucking engagement party, he's going to her.

"What does she need?" I ask, but my question is masked by the ringing of his phone.

"I love you." He presses a kiss to my forehead and pulls his phone from his pocket. "Hey... Yeah, I'm on my way."

Then he's out the door.

I watch him jog down the stairs, the phone to his ear the whole time. When he disappears around the corner, I return to my apartment. *Breathe. Just breathe.*

But the reminder doesn't help, and I have to rush to the bathroom to throw up.

I never thought I'd be engaged to a man I couldn't trust. I never thought I would doubt Max of all people. He hasn't done anything to deserve my suspicion, but I can't help it. The old insecurity is back, and it doesn't matter what I look like now or how many pounds I lost, because Meredith is everything I'll never be. Blond, slim, the kind of woman men's eyes go to when she enters a room.

And to top it off, she's a complete bitch. William Bailey dated her for a while before Cally came back in town, and when he broke it off for his first love, Meredith got artificially inseminated and let everyone in town think it was Will's baby.

After brushing my teeth and settling my angry stomach with Sprite, I found my underwear—so much for *that* seduction plan— and a pair of canvas flats and started walking.

Nothing calms me like the sound of the river, so I hit the path behind the bakery. Three times, I've pulled up Max's number on my phone, ready to call him and demand answers. Three times, I've changed my mind. I don't want to be *that girl*. Insecure. Untrusting. He's marrying me, isn't he? And if he were doing something wrong, would he have told me where he was going?

I pull off my shoes and walk in the cool grass, the stars mocking me from above with their happy twinkling. I don't know how long I walk or how far, but by the time I've left the center of town and can see my mom's house in the distance, the bottoms of my feet are raw from walking barefoot.

In front of me lies the empty expanse of Mom's backyard. The party is over. The band's been packed up, the decorations taken down. All like it never existed.

I'm not ready to return to my apartment yet, so I stop at the dock just between Mom's and Asher's adjoining properties.

I sink onto the wooden planks, wrap my arms around my knees, lean my head against them, and tell myself everything is going to be okay.

I focus on breathing. *In. And out. In. And out.*

"You planning on sleeping there or just staying long enough to ruin that sexy dress?"

I lift my head to see a dark figure leaning against the rail at the end of the dock. I blink until Nate Crane comes into focus. He takes a drag off a cigarette—no, not a cigarette, a joint. I sneer in disgust. I hate drugs. I have no use for people who can't think of any better way to entertain themselves.

"You planning on getting stoned the rest of your life or actually doing something meaningful?"

He steps closer, and in the light of the moon, I can make out the half smirk, half smile on his lips. "Asher and Maggie invited me to your engagement party tonight, but I decided being stoned and useless would be more enjoyable. So would Chinese water torture, come to think of it. Looks like maybe you feel the same." He takes another step closer and offers the joint.

"Fuck no." I wave away the puff of smoke left behind and cough for good measure.

"Suit yourself," he murmurs. He shifts his gaze back to the river, but instead of taking another drag, he pinches off the glowing tip into the water and tucks the rest into his pocket. "Do you want to talk about it?"

"I don't know what you're talking about." I sound like a sulking teenager.

He arches a brow but doesn't press.

Releasing my knees, I pull myself up and stand beside him at the rail. "That first weekend we met, did I tell you about how much I wanted to open a bakery?"

"You did."

I have to ask. "And you wanted me to do it?"

"I told you I thought you should." A frog sings in the distance, filling the silence. "You have talent."

"I love it, you know. Every time I walk in, I smile."

"Glad to hear it." There's a rough, pained edge to his words.

"And you made sure I had a chance," I say matter-of-factly.

"I'm not sure what you mean."

Clearly he's not interested in changing the "anonymous" part of our arrangement, and I'm too grateful to push the issue, but I can't help the sigh that slips from my lips. "I feel like everyone knows more about my life than I do."

He looks out over the water. "What do you want to know?"

"Everything," I whisper.

"Why?" If an open wound has a sound, it's the sound of his voice right now.

"You have no idea what it's like to be missing pieces of your memory, to feel like your own body is failing you."

He grunts. "Do you remember anything from our time together?"

"Nothing."

"Will it come back?"

The wind shifts, and a cloud blocks the moon and cloaks us in darkness. I'm standing in the dark with a man who's a stranger to me. I should be uncomfortable—cautious at the very least. Instead, my muscles relax incrementally. There's something comforting about darkness, about not being seen.

"The doctor says it's hard to say at this point," I say. "Maybe, maybe not. The closer the memory is to the time of my accident, the less likely I am to remember it. Maybe I won't ever remember you. Maybe if you hadn't climbed into bed with me two weeks ago, I'd never have known about us."

"My life's biggest regret," he murmurs.

I wince. If he'd slapped me, it would have hurt less. "I'm your biggest regret?"

"No." He growls the word then takes a breath. "I'm not this great guy. I've made a lot of mistakes. Done a lot of shitty things, made a lot of selfish choices. But in the end, it's all worked out."

I wish I could see his face, read the nuance of his expression.

Instead, he's only a silhouette in the night, and I'm left with nothing but his words and the low rumble of his voice.

"I don't regret much," he explains. "But I do regret crawling into bed with you when I came to town." He looks to the sky. "Your amnesia was a gift that I fucked up."

"You *wanted* me to forget you?"

His chest expands on his inhale, and I have to fight this irrational desire to lean my head against him. To comfort him with my presence, despite what he's saying. "It would be…easier."

"I'm not going to bother you, if that's what you're worried about. I won't be the girl who runs to the tabloids to tell about her hot night with Nate Crane."

"Hanna." He takes my shoulders and turns me to face him. He studies me for a beat. Two. Like he's trying to solve a puzzle and the answer is in my eyes. Then he drops his hands and turns away again. While he stares out into the stillness of the night, I'm left to guess what he might have been about to say.

"I might not remember what happened between us, but I feel something…" I make a fist and press it to my chest. "Something here. Every time you're close."

"And what about him? Do you feel it when he's close?"

Hot tears sting the backs of my eyes and I nod. "I do."

"There's your answer." His gaze settles on my hand, his eyes burning into the ring on my finger. "That's all you need to know."

"But I don't even remember putting it on. How can I trust a decision I don't remember making?" My question is punctuated by a distant owl call.

"You're the smartest girl I know. I trust your decision. Maybe you should too."

"I need to know something first."

He hangs his head. "You should talk to your fiancé."

"Did I sleep with you?"

The clouds shift again, and the moonlight casts shadows on the beautiful hard angles of his face. My heart pounds hard as he steps closer. He tilts my chin up until my eyes are on his.

"What do you think?"

"I think we all make mistakes."

Something flashes in his eyes, but it's gone as quickly as it appeared, his expression whitewashed by that stoner-may-care blankness.

I have to repeat the question. If I don't, I might lose my nerve and run away without hearing the answer. "Did we have sex?"

"No. We didn't."

There's no relief at his words. Not really. Only emptiness. Any way you paint it, I still betrayed my fiancé. I've been promising myself I'd tell Max the truth if I learned that I slept with Nate. Maybe I wanted the excuse to confess.

"Goodnight, angel."

"Don't go."

He closes his eyes, and I can't help myself anymore. I touch his face, carefully, tentatively. He stands stock-still as I skim my fingertips over the rough stubble of his cheek, study him while his eyes are closed. Then I just hold there, neither of us moving or breathing. Caught in the moment and the moonlight.

When he opens his eyes, they're filled with pain. With longing. Is that real, or am I seeing what I want to believe? He's as much a mystery to me as this connection between us.

He parts his lips and his eyes lock with mine. Just when I think we might stand here forever, a tragic tableau of secrets and heartache, he shifts a fraction of an inch and leans into my touch.

"Dammit, Hanna." The words are soft, tortured. "What do you want me to do?"

"Kiss me." And I can't believe what I'm asking, but the command is out there and I can't take it back. I don't want to.

"How am I supposed to say no to that?"

"You're not."

His gaze dips to my lips, and my heart races. A pace so painful and violent I fear it might burst from my chest right here and fall to his feet.

As his mouth moves toward mine, a sense of calm washes over me. My shoulders drop. My breathing slows. For a moment, my past doesn't matter. My future doesn't matter. Only here. Only now.

When his lips are so close I can almost taste him, he squeezes his eyes shut and leans his forehead against mine. "I love you too much to screw this up for you. I love you too much to let you beat yourself up over a stupid kiss." He staggers back.

"I'm sorry." My hand goes to my mouth. Shame washes over me, a hot rush followed by the icy-cold grip of loneliness. "I shouldn't have... I don't know why—"

"Go home, Hanna. Go be with your future husband."

Chapter
FOURTEEN

"HAS ANYONE ever told you that you work too much?" Max asks as the front door swings closed behind him.

I hand Mrs. Oaks her non-fat cappuccino and smile for her benefit as I say, "Takes one to know one."

She smiles back. "Could I also have the rest of your cheese Danishes, sweetheart?"

"Of course!" I grab a box off the shelf behind me and fill it.

"I'm going to surprise the ladies at Bible study with them," Mrs. Oaks says as I ring her up. "I brought them chocolate croissants last week, and you'd have thought I brought them each a piece of the moon."

"You're too sweet!"

"It's all true." She pays and tucks the box under her arm. "You two have a lovely day. Tell your mom I said hi, Hanna."

"I will. Thanks."

Max steps behind the counter as the woman leaves. We're alone in the front, only us and the sounds of Drew doing cleanup in the kitchen. He slips his hands under my shirt from behind me and draws me against him.

I tense.

Nuzzling the side of my neck, he takes a long, deep breath.

"You smell like clean sheets and flowers," he murmurs. "I just want to breathe you in for days."

The heat of his mouth against the side of my neck should be sweet and delicious, but instead it makes my stomach hurt. "You're distracting me," I protest lamely.

"Mission accomplished." His hand moves farther north and cups my breast, and even as part of my body reacts, warming and purring for more, another part of me is thinking about Nate. The way his whispers sent an electric buzz of pleasure through my veins last night. The regret in his eyes as he pulled away.

Max must sense something, because his hands still and he takes his mouth off my neck. "Are we okay?"

Three words. A simple question. My throat grows thick. "I didn't like the way you ran off to be with Meredith last night. It hurt me."

He withdraws, pulls his hands out from under my shirt, and steps back. "I didn't go off to *be with her*. It's not like that."

I set my jaw and cross my arms over my chest. I don't want to know his reasons or what kind of emergency she had. "It made me feel like I was less important to you than she is."

He exhales heavily and drags a hand through his hair. "I'm sorry you felt that way."

"That's not an apology." I spin and push into the kitchen. All my life I've struggled with telling people when their actions hurt me, and all too often it meant being used and trampled. The reason my twin sister is my closest friend is because she doesn't need to be told when I hurt. She can tell without me saying it.

I grab a tray and fill it with snickerdoodles from the cooling rack.

"I was just about to do that," Drew says, hands on her hips. She took the early baking shift this morning—thank God, since it was after two when I finally got to bed.

"I got it," I mutter.

"Don't let your shitty mood ruin my hard work," she grouses.

"Drew," I hear Max say, "can you cover the front so I can talk to Hanna?"

"Trouble in paradise?" she asks, but when I glare at her, she throws up her hands and scurries to the front.

"Did I miss something?" he asks. He crosses to me and turns me to face him.

Instead of meeting his eyes, I stare at his cheesy gym logo on his chest: *Hallowell Health Club, Fitness to the Max.*

"What's really going on here?"

I close my eyes. I feel so childish, like the teenager who throws a fit when she sees her boyfriend talking to another girl. "I remembered Valentine's Day," I admit.

"Valentine's Day?" He looks lost.

"You left to help Meredith." I shake my head. "I understand that I might seem irrationally jealous, but trust takes time to build. You have almost nine months of our relationship to lean on when you have a bad day. I have two weeks and a handful of memories. Last night made me feel unimportant, and I didn't like that."

His hard jaw softens. "I'm sorry."

"I'm not saying you can't help out a friend, but I need to know—I need to believe—I matter."

"Of course you do." He runs his finger over my cheek. "You're my life, Hanna. My future. You matter."

When he lowers his lips to mine, my anger has melted into a puddle at my feet. Maybe this shouldn't be the end of this fight. Maybe I should press the issue. But I'm so confused after last night that I just want the security of his touch. I let him kiss me and I kiss him back until the last of my hurt has evaporated into the sweet, sugar-scented air of the kitchen.

"You love birds can't keep your hands off each other, can you?"

The sound of my mother's voice has me breaking the kiss and backing away. She's already sipping a cup of coffee, her Bible tucked under her arm.

"Good morning, Mom. How was church?"

"Wonderful. Just wonderful. I wanted to invite you and Max to Sunday brunch. Max, a few of the ladies from the New Hope Restoration Council will be there. Don't get me wrong, I think we're going to get you that grant for your gym—I've really been pulling for you—but it couldn't hurt to schmooze. A little insurance, you know."

This is the first I've heard of Max applying for a grant with the city restoration group, but I'm not surprised. Mom sits on the board, and it makes sense that they would give one of their grants to a business like Max's.

"I can't, Mom. I have too much to do here."

"You work too much," she says.

Max grins and winks at me. "That's what I keep telling her."

"Max, why don't you go without me? Mom's right. It certainly wouldn't be a bad idea to get some face time."

He nods and steals a cookie off the tray. "I can come by for a bit."

Mom brightens. "Wonderful! While you're there, I'll introduce you to Fred Wellings. He's the contractor who built my house. Built William Bailey's too. You can talk to him about building you and Hanna a house after your wedding."

Max lowers the cookie that was halfway to his mouth, cutting his eyes to me and then back to Mom. "Mrs. Thompson, Hanna and I both have new businesses. We're really not going to be in a position to build a house for quite a while."

"Balderdash," Mom says, waving her hand. "Hanna will get her trust fund once she's married. There's plenty there to build a home and have a little nest egg."

Poor Max looks so uncomfortable.

"We're going to live in my apartment for a while," I say.

"That will be great for while you're building, of course, but you can't raise my grandbabies in a tiny apartment above your bakery."

Max and I exchange and glance. "We'll talk about it," I promise.

She looks at her watch and squeaks. "I need to get going. Max, I'll see you at the house later."

When she's finally gone, I turn to him and wince. "I'm sorry. She totally blindsided me with that, but that's pretty much Mom's MO."

He takes my hands and squeezes my fingers. "It's okay. Maybe we'll talk about it later."

I nod. "I never really think about my trust fund. That's money from Daddy's insurance. If he hadn't died so young, it wouldn't be nearly what it is, so it's not really something I like to think about.

She's right, though. There's enough there for us to build a nice house if that's what we want to do."

"Well." He tilts his head, his eyes searching my face. "I guess it all depends on how soon you want to give her those grandbabies she's talking about."

"I—oh, um… I'm not sure I'm ready to be a mom yet. I mean, we're young still, right? And…" *And if I get pregnant, I'm going to get fat again, and what if you don't want me anymore?*

"Okay." He squeezes my hands again, but the gesture isn't reassuring when everything about his expression tells me I didn't give him the answer he was hoping for.

"So how are you feeling?" Nix asks when I'm sitting in her office on Wednesday morning.

"I've been nauseated a couple times, but I think it's just stress. You know, weddings," I say lamely.

"How are the headaches?"

"I haven't had a headache in probably a week."

"That's great news." She looks in my eyes and ears. "And you said you're getting some of your memories back?"

"Some," I say, "not all. It's frustrating, but I'm trying to be patient."

"What about the other thing we talked about in the hospital?"

I raise a brow.

"Do you feel safe?" She pauses a beat. "Is Max good to you?"

"Oh! Of course." I wave my hand. "Seriously, I'm sure I just fell down the stairs. Max is a prince."

She frowns. "Your sister says you've been spending time with her and Maggie again, not isolating yourself like you had been. That's a good sign."

"Of course. Other than Cally, my sisters are my best friends."

"Keep that up. It's important that you have a support system, not just Max."

"I will. I promise."

She nods, looking satisfied. "Did you fast this morning?"

I wince. "Crap. I totally forgot you wanted to do blood work."

"That's okay." She smiles and lowers herself into her chair. "You can swing by the lab any morning to get that done, but I can guess already that it's going to look better."

"Why do you say that?"

"Well, in the two and a half weeks since you've been out of the hospital, you've gained about six pounds. I know without seeing your lab work that you're eating again. That's good news."

"You're the first doctor who's ever called my weight gain good news." I can't handle the sympathy in her sad smile, so I study the blue specks on the industrial-grade flooring tiles. "Did you know? About the anorexia?"

Nix takes a breath, surprised at my confession, I guess. "I suspected, but you weren't very receptive when I tried to talk to you about it over the summer."

"Do you think I can start working out again? Running?"

"Let's start with a week of light, low-impact workouts. If that goes okay, you can try a short run. Just ease back in and listen to your body. But I don't want you working out more than once a day, got it?"

"I'm scared I'm going to gain it all back." I hate admitting this. I hate letting someone see how much my stupid body affects how I feel about myself. "But I think I'm just as scared of letting food control my life, letting my desire to be thin ruin everything else." When I lift my head to meet her gaze, there's more understanding in her eyes than I expected.

"You're probably going to put on some more weight, at least some of it. When you lose weight in such an unhealthy way, your body can't maintain it when you go back to eating and exercising normally. There will be an adjustment period where you figure out what weight you can maintain while eating regularly and having a healthy relationship with exercise."

I nod, but my eyes fill and I have to look away. I only have a few recovered memories of Nix, and I don't know how close we are. But if I voice my fears to Liz, she'll just be mad at me.

"What is it, Hanna?"

The floor's blue specks swim before my eyes. A tear plops onto the tile next to my sandaled foot. "What if the weight comes back and Max isn't attracted to me anymore?"

"Oh, sweetie." Then she surprises me by hugging me, wrapping me up against her.

"Are doctors supposed to hug their patients?" I ask, hugging her back awkwardly.

"I'm not hugging you as your doctor. I'm hugging you as your friend." She squeezes one more time before releasing me. "You need to talk to Max. You can't live the rest of your life fearing that he might not want you."

May—Three Months Before Accident

"I'm so pleased to meet you, Miss Thompson," the lawyer says. She gestures to the chair and takes her seat on the other side of her desk. "I'm sure you're wondering why I summoned you."

"I am." I lower myself into the wingback chair. Her office is slick and modern with just enough homey touches—throw pillows, framed snapshots—to make it comfortable. Well, to make most people comfortable. There's nothing comfortable about how I feel being called to Indianapolis to meet with a lawyer I've never heard of before. "I can only assume I have a distant rich relative who passed away and left me his fortune."

She laughs good-naturedly. "I keep waiting for that call myself, but unfortunately, that's not why you're here today."

"Bummer." I force a smile and shift in my chair. Waiting.

"I understand you just graduated from Sinclair and have a successful side business decorating cakes for friends."

"I did just graduate, though I'm not sure how successful I'd call my business. I do it more for fun than anything."

"You enjoy it, then?"

"Of course!" My cheeks warm. "It's fun to make something out of raw ingredients. And cakes just make people happy."

"And you have a dream of opening up your own bakery in

New Hope. Is that correct?"

This will definitely be filed under Strangest Experiences Ever. "Yes, but it's really more of a pipe dream. Nothing serious."

"What if it didn't have to be a pipe dream?" She pushes a thin stack of papers across the desk. "My client who, let's be clear from the start, wishes to remain anonymous, thinks your 'pipe dream' bakery plans, as you call them, could really turn into a profitable venture."

I pick up the stack of papers and leaf through them, but I'm not really sure what I'm looking at.

"The one on the top is the New Hope revitalization project, explaining tax breaks and grant funds the town of New Hope will give to young entrepreneurs who want to help revitalize the historic square."

I scan the page, my eyes landing on the maximum dollar amounts the city will contribute. "I know about these grants," I say, nodding. "William Bailey got some grant money to open his art gallery. I'm familiar with the opportunities, but they aren't anything near what someone like me would need to open my own business." I'd be able to do it with the money in my trust fund, but I don't get that until I'm thirty or married.

Max's proposal flashes through my mind—the look on his face when I stared at the ring and didn't speak, the moment he rose off his knee and placed the ring in my hand, closing my fingers around it. *"Keep it. That's how much I want this, Hanna. Keep it. I'll wait."*

What was the "this" that he wanted? Me or my trust fund? I squeeze my eyes shut.

"That's why I'm here. My client would like to go into business with you, Hanna. He would provide the rest of the funds you need to open the bakery in the old Woolworth's building on Main. We've had a team of contractors give us estimates on turning around the space, and he'd even put an apartment for you upstairs to compensate for the minimal income you'd expect your first months in business."

"How can I go into business with someone who wants to remain anonymous?"

"He'd be a silent partner. He'd get a portion of your profits until you choose to buy him out or sell the business."

"But what if I don't make a profit? What's in it for him then?"

She shrugs. "Investments always come with risk, but my client believes you'll be successful."

"So if I want to make a decision, how am I supposed to talk to him?"

"Most things you'd be free to decide on your own, but there are major decisions he'd want to be consulted on, and those would go through me."

Who would want to go into business with me? Who do I know with the money to take on something like this? "Is Nate Crane behind this?"

Her face remains impassive. "Anonymous means anonymous."

It has to be Nate. And I should say no. I shouldn't accept his money. Only he's offering me something I want so badly. I can already picture my bakery on Main, Sinclair students hopping in between classes for a gourmet coffee, a glass case with freshly baked cookies and scones.

"Do you think you'd like to talk more, or is an anonymous partnership out of the question for you?"

"Tell me more."

Chapter
FIFTEEN

AT FIRST, I'm not sure if what I'm hearing is someone knocking on my door because the booming thunder of the storm masks it. Then it comes again. *Boom, boom, boom.*

I slide my laptop onto the couch beside me and rush to the door.

"Hanna?" Liz calls.

"What are you doing out in this storm?" I hurry to the door and yank it open.

Liz steps in, soaking wet but grinning. Maggie, Cally, and Nix pile in right behind her. "Impromptu girls' night!" Liz announces.

"Sorry, I couldn't hear the knocking over the thunder."

The girls shed their shoes and jackets by the door, and I grab towels for them.

"It's a mess out there," my sister says. She wipes the rain from her face and shakes her curls, not unlike a dog coming in from the rain.

Cally goes into the kitchen and plugs her iPod into the radio, and Maggie hoists a couple of canvas shopping bags on the counter and starts pulling out cream, Godiva liqueur, and vodka—ingredients for chocolate martinis, if I'm not mistaken. Nix removes a box of truffles, cheese, and crackers from another bag.

"You guys," I say. "I have a wedding dress to fit into in three and a half weeks."

Liz opens cabinet doors until she finds my martini glasses and sets them on the island. "You've never had us over here."

"We had to remedy that," Cally says, grinning.

"And Asher and Nate are working like fiends, so I was bored," Maggie explains.

"Where's Will?" I ask Cally.

"He's hanging with Max and Sam at Brady's."

I head to the island and pop a truffle in my mouth. "That is amazing!" I close my eyes and chew slowly.

"God, it's good to see you eat!" Cally says as she chooses a chocolate. "You were losing weight so fast. I was worried about you."

"She's doing really well," Nix says. She winks at me as she grabs a truffle for herself. "Oh, wow!"

"They're orgasmic, aren't they?" Maggie says. "Asher got them for me when he was in New York last month. There's this shop in the city that I swear does voodoo to make their chocolate."

"Let me try." Lizzy abandons her half-made chocolate martinis to try the orgasmic treat for herself. "Holy shit! I didn't know chocolate could be *better*."

The speakers click as Cally's iPod shuffles to a new song, and Nate Crane's "Lost In Me" begins.

I gasp.

Lizzy reaches over and squeezes my hand, and I close my eyes.

"That's it." Maggie slaps her palm on the counter. "What is going on with Nate Crane?"

Lizzy puts on her innocent face. "What do you mean?"

"Something's up with you two. You get all weird any time I mention Nate, and he gets all weird every time I say anything about my sisters."

"Weird?" Lizzy says. "We're just fans. That's all."

Maggie raises a disbelieving brow. "You are a shitty liar."

My twin sighs dramatically. "Fine. You know how I feel about his hotness. You caught me. I'm sleeping with Nate Crane."

"You wish," Maggie mutters before she zeroes in on me.

"Hanna, spill."

"She doesn't—"

I hold up a hand. It was only a matter of time, right? "It's okay. I made this mess and now I have to live with the consequences. Maggie should know."

"It started in St. Louis, didn't it?" She looks heartbroken.

"She doesn't have her memory, remember?" Lizzy defends.

"I don't know much. But the night I got home from the hospital, I woke up with Nate in my bed, and he was really angry when he saw my ring."

"Jesus." Cally drags her hand over her face.

"You can't say anything to Will," I plead with her. "Not until I tell Max the truth."

"You haven't told Max?" Nix says.

"Amnesia, remember?" Liz says. "She can't even remember being with him."

"But he climbed into your bed," Maggie points out. "Did you ask him what's been going on between you?"

"He's not real keen on talking to her," Liz says. "You know, given that she chose the other guy."

"But you know for sure there was something going on between the two of you?" Maggie asks. "You and *Nate Crane*?"

"You're one to talk," Liz retorts. "You're fucking Asher Logan. Seriously, what's happened to this town? And when do I get a sultry affair with a sexy rocker?"

Nix shakes her head as if to clear it and grabs the martini shaker from Lizzy's hand. She pulls off the top and takes a drink straight from the shaker. "No wonder you're so anxious for those memories to come back," she mutters. "*I'm* anxious for you to get those memories back."

"I know, right?" Liz says. "I want details, and whether she remembers or not, I'm pretty sure I'm never going to get them."

"What about Max?" Worry is written all over Cally's face. "You *are* going to tell him, right?"

"I have to," I whisper.

"Hanna!" Lizzy says.

"I've made up my mind, Liz. I'm giving my brain one more

week to share any details it has hidden in there and then I'm telling Max what I know. For better or worse."

Liz exhales heavily. "You're stressing me out. Thank God we have chocolate." She pops another truffle into her mouth and moans again as she chews. "Oh, hell, that's better than sex."

"No, it's not," Cally and Maggie say in unison. Then they giggle, and Maggie nudges me. "Come on. Don't make me feel like the dirty ho here. I know you guys agree with me. That chocolate is good, but it's *not* better than sex."

"I wouldn't remember," Lizzy says. She takes the martini shaker back from Nix and takes a gulp.

"Sisters in unwanted abstinence," Nix says.

Lizzy gives her a high five. "An exclusive club that no one wants to join."

"Tell me about it," I mutter.

The girls stare at me, and Liz bites back a laugh. "Hanna just found out she and Max don't have sex. She's not taking it very well."

Maggie's eyes go wide. "But you're, like, twenty-three. And you and Max have been together for *months*. How does that even happen?"

"She's saving herself for marriage," Lizzy says. "Who knew any of the Thompson girls would make it to marriage with her virginity? Mom would be so proud."

"So you weren't having sex with Nate Crane?" Cally asks.

"Apparently not," I say.

"How do you know?" Nix asks quietly.

"I saw him over the weekend and asked. He said we didn't." I frown. "You're my doctor. What do you know about this that I'm not remembering?"

Nix breaks a cracker in half and avoids my eyes. "We can have this conversation in private later."

"I want to have it now. These ladies already know my worst secret. Tell me what you know."

She holds up her hands in defense. "Nothing, really. I was not privy to the details of your sex life. And you certainly never told me you were involved with Nate Crane, sexually or otherwise."

"But…" I prod.

"But you came in at the beginning of August and talked to me about birth-control options. You'd had some problems with headaches when you were on hormonal contraceptives in high school, so you wanted to know about some other options and decided that condoms and a diaphragm was the right combination for you."

"So I got a diaphragm?"

"We fitted you for one."

"Did I tell you anything else?"

She breaks another cracker and sweeps a small pile of crumbs in front of her. "You were still a virgin when we talked, according to you. But you didn't think…"

"You're killing me with the suspense," Liz says. "She didn't think what?"

Nix shrugs. "She didn't think she'd make it more than a couple more weeks."

"That doesn't mean anything," Cally says. "She could have been planning to sleep with Max."

Thunder claps, and half a second later, the apartment goes black, blessedly ending the awkward conversation.

"Candles," I announce. "I'll find candles. And…matches or something."

I hear a click, and the next thing I know, a single flame is illuminating my friends' faces from the lighter in Nix's hand. "I've got us halfway there."

"You carry a lighter?"

"And a pocketknife," she says proudly. "I had four Eagle Scouts for big brothers. Always be prepared and all that jazz."

"Do you need help looking for the candles?" Liz asks.

"No. I know where to look."

I head toward the bedroom, my mind still churning on the implications of what Nix just told me. If I was getting birth control only a couple of weeks before the accident, that could mean I'd decided to accept Max's proposal. Or it could mean I'd decided to earn my scarlet letter after all.

"They're not in the kitchen?" Maggie calls, and I can already hear her opening drawers and rummaging through them.

"Maybe, but I know I store scented candles in my drawers. They work better than sachets for keeping clothes smelling fresh."

"She's so girly," Nix says. "I need you guys to teach me how to be girly. Could you? For my birthday?"

I feel my way to my dresser and pull open the top drawer. Fumbling through piles of cotton and satin and lace, I finally find what I'm looking for. "Found one! It's a taper candle, so we'll have to hold it until we can find a candleholder, but this should get us started."

As I leave the bedroom, lightning flashes and floods the apartment for two beats. Then we're left in darkness again.

I fumble with the candle as I scoot my way back toward the kitchen. It's kind of an odd shape. I wonder if it melted in the heat and re-formed or something. I hope no wax melted on my undies. "Nix, can you light your lighter again? I can't find the wick."

With a metallic click, the lighter blazes, and I lift the candle. "Do you see the wick anywhere?"

The room fills with Lizzy's peals of laughter. "What drawer was that in?"

My cheeks heat. "My underwear drawer."

"Lemme guess. It was tucked under your lingerie, maybe some sexy undies?" Even in the faint flickering of Nix's lighter, I can see glee written all over Liz's face.

"Oh. My. God." As the realization hits me, my hand opens and I release the *oh-my-God-that's-no-candle*. It falls to the floor with a thump.

Liz sinks to her haunches and picks it up off the floor with two fingers, the way one might hold a pair of someone else's dirty underwear.

"It looks like a taper candle in the dark," I say. "I don't even know where that came from."

Maggie snorts. "Amnesia is *such* a handy excuse now, isn't it?"
Kill me now.

"Is it…is it what I think it is?" Nix asks.

"I guess that depends what you think it is," Liz says. Twisting it at its center, she confirms my worst suspicions and sends it into a vibrating tizzy.

I back away. Horrified.

Lizzy giggles harder. "It doesn't bite."

"I didn't even know I had a... Why do I have that?"

My mind wraps around the words from the texts on Nate's phone. Nate asking if I'd taken my gift home. What had I replied? *"It's a sorry substitute for you"*?

Not just a vibrator. Worse. A vibrator that was a gift from Nate.

The girls are all giggling now.

"I know you two are close," Cally says, "but I absolutely cannot believe you're touching that."

"I don't get it," Nix says. "She gets buff, sexy-ass Max Hallowell and an affair with the sexy rocker. What's the need for the vibrating friend, Hanna?"

If the floor wanted to open up and swallow me right now, I'd be okay with that.

Another flash lights the room. I must look as horrified as I feel, because Lizzy's giggles go quiet. "Hanna, we're just giving you a hard time. Are you okay?"

"I'll go find your candles," Maggie says, taking the lighter from Nix.

I watch her silhouette move through the darkness and into my bedroom. I shouldn't let her rifle through my clothes—God knows what else she might find that I don't know about—but another flash of lightning fills the space and a memory comes with it. Not the memory of sending those texts to Nate. A different memory. Clear and vivid and visceral.

Maggie is carrying a lit candle in each hand when she returns.

"We'll stop teasing you about the vibrator," Nix promises me. "We all have one."

"Those bitches probably don't," Liz says, pointing to Cally and Maggie. She tosses the vibrator onto the island. Right there between the truffles and cheese. "They have men to do that work for them."

Maggie snorts. "Where have you been, Liz? Men and vibrators go very well together."

"She's not lying," Cally says.

"I hate you all," Liz growls.

"Can we change the subject?" The question comes out of me with an awkward squeak.

"Sure," Nix says. "Let's talk about what we're going to do for Cally's bachelorette party."

The girls start chattering about their plans and ideas, but I can't seem to focus on the conversation. My mind is playing and replaying the memory of Nate Crane's wicked eyes watching me as he rubs the vibrator over my inner thighs.

"What do you think, Hanna?" Lizzy asks.

"Um, what?" *Stop thinking about the vibrator. Stop thinking about Nate holding the vibrator.*

Maggie laughs. "We're trying to decide whether or not we should crash Will's bachelor party. He's not going to be able to talk Sam out of the strip club, so we're thinking we should show up."

"Oh, that could be fun." *Stop thinking about Nate Crane.*

But it's useless. I finally have a memory of Nate Crane, and instead of helping me let him go, I'm so wrapped up in it I feel lost and confused all over again.

June—Two Months Before Accident

The ribbon-wrapped box sits on the crisp white linens of the hotel bed, and I creep toward it, unable to resist the lure of an unexpected gift.

Strong arms encase me from behind, and I feel Nate's breath hot in my ear. "I got you something." His mouth drops to my neck, where he nibbles his way down to my shoulder and sends little shivers whipping through me.

I close my eyes against the pleasure and moan. "I saw that. You shouldn't have."

"Hmm," he groans, his hands already sliding inside my shirt. "You shouldn't say that until you know what it is. It might be more for me than it is for you." His fingers skim over my belly then slide into the band of my jeans and sweep lower, sending my knees weak. "You want to open it?"

"You're kind of making me want something else right now."

He chuckles and nips my neck one last time before pulling away and grabbing the box off the bed.

"You should stop buying me things," I protest lamely.

"Don't steal my joy, woman." He nudges the gift toward me, and I take it in my hands and pull off the lid.

I'd like to pretend I'm one of those worldly girls who doesn't shock or embarrass easily, but I'm not. The gift inside this box both shocks and embarrasses me, but I make myself pick it up and hold it in my hand as I say, "Thank you?" Unfortunately, any attempt at sincerity is lost when the words come out like a question.

He chuckles. "You don't sound like you mean it."

"Um, no, I do mean it. Thanks." I put the box down on the bed and study the object. "I just… I'm not sure why…"

"It's a vibrator, Hanna. Not a medieval torture device." He steps closer and closes my hand over the toy, twisting its shaft under my fingers.

"Oh!" I squeak when it starts buzzing in my hands, but he holds tight, keeping my fingers wrapped around it. A giggle slips from my lips. "Um…should I be worried that you said this is more for you than me? I mean, I'm game to try new things, but I've never been with a guy who wanted—"

He grunts. "Not like that."

"No. I want to give you what you want. Um…" I motion toward the bed and bite my lip as laughter bubbles up in my chest. "Bend over?"

He grins and steps closer. "I have other plans, but thanks for the offer. Means a lot."

"I'm very open-minded," I say sagely.

"Your face when you opened it doesn't support that claim. Have you ever used one of these before?"

My lips part as his hands lead mine over the vibrating shaft in long, lewd movements that kind of turn me on. "I guess I would just prefer the real thing. You know. If someone would give it to me." I pout. "It's the least you could do when you're going to be leaving me for the Middle East in September."

"I promise, having sex now wouldn't make a month apart any

easier."

My shoulders sag. "I hate that you're going. I'm going to be worried sick until you're home safe."

He groans and nips at my ear. His hot lips sweep over my neck and then his hands slip under my shirt, making circles around my navel. "You're cute when you're worried about me. Now get naked and lay your sweet ass on that bed so I can show you just what I want you to do with this."

"Oh." I grin and unbutton my jeans, watching him as I push them off my hips. I leave my panties and T-shirt on and climb onto the bed. "In that case…"

"You're not naked."

I lift a brow. "Neither are you." I love his hot eyes on me.

"Lie down."

I obey, and he runs his eyes over me again and again. Nate looking at me is as good as any foreplay I've ever known.

He hands me the vibrator then moves to the end of the bed. "Put it between your legs."

"I'd rather you do it for me," I protest. Turning the device in my hands, I look up at him through my lashes. I know how badly he wants to touch me, how much self-restraint he's using to stay at the foot of the bed when he could be on the bed with me. Touching me.

"You're going to have to figure out how to use it yourself." He folds his arms and stares down at me like a warden supervising his charge.

I grin. "You think I don't know how to get myself off? Aren't you cute?"

A muscle in his jaw jumps, but he raises a brow and holds my gaze. "Prove it."

My heart leaps into my throat at the challenge, and I lick my lips. When I part my legs, his nostrils flare and his eyes go darker. "With this?" I ask, holding up the vibrator.

"Show me how you do it." He drops his arms and his fists clench at his sides.

I release the vibrator on the bed next to me. Keeping my eyes on him, I cup myself between my legs. I'm so turned on from all this talk of masturbation and the look in his eyes. I'm already slick and swollen, and if he joined me on the bed and put his hand between my legs, he could get me off in seconds flat.

But he isn't on the bed with me, and I'm not going to rush this. I rock my hand against myself, applying just enough pressure to my clit to make my eyes float closed.

"Here." His hard voice has my eyes flying open. He's leaning over the bed and tugging my panties from my hips in one smooth motion.

I squeak as my ass falls back to the bed, and he gives me that shit-eating grin.

"You have touched yourself without the panties before, haven't you?"

I take a breath and part my legs farther. He watches, and that's what does it for me—his gaze between my legs, like that private bit of me is the most beautiful thing he's ever seen, the rising and falling of his chest as I slide my hands up my inner thighs.

I've never done this before—never let a man watch me touch myself. I would have thought it would be awkward or that I'd worry I might look like I was enjoying my own touch more that I enjoyed his, but there's nothing awkward here, and we both know it's Nate's touch I want. All I feel is heat and lust and this need to give him anything he wants.

As I settle on hand over myself, taking my clit between two fingers, I bring my other hand up to my chest and squeeze my breast through my shirt. I'm not wearing a bra, and the sensation of my sensitive nipples scraping across the cotton makes my hips buck and my body ache for more. For his mouth on my breasts, his tongue toying with my nipples until he draws them into his mouth—hard and tight and merciless.

I enter myself with one finger as I imagine it, and he steps closer. I love that I can make him damn near lose his self-control. I imagine his mouth against the flat of my belly before dipping lower.

I squeeze my clit gently. Right where I want his lips. My hips rock faster and his eyes grow hotter.

I'm close. So damn close. But my own hand isn't enough when he's right there, when I can reach out and touch what I really want. "Nate," I whimper.

"Do it, angel." His nostrils flare as I pinch my nipple through my shirt again. "I want to hear you come. I want to watch."

"I want you to do it."

"Do this for me." His breathing is ragged. As if he's been holding me up and fucking me hard rather than standing here watching.

I can see what I'm doing to him. I can see it in his eyes, hear it in his voice.

"Fuck your hand for me, baby. Just like that." His words make me wild and my hips move faster, my hand at my breast pinches tighter, and then I'm gone—tightening, squeezing, and exploding into a hard and fast release that's better than any orgasm I've ever been able to give myself.

As I lie limp in bed after, he climbs in beside me and brushes my hair from my face. "I swear to Christ, you are a living fantasy."

I force my heavy eyes open. "That was amazing. I wouldn't have believed I could make myself…"

"Get off?"

I shake my head. "I knew I could do that, but it's never that good. But with you standing there…"

He presses a kiss to the side of my neck. "That's what I want you to think about when I'm gone. When you touch yourself, imagine me at the end of the bed watching you."

I hear the hum of the vibrator clicking on, and then he's pressing it against the inside of my thighs and sucking at my neck as he inches the vibrating wand closer to the apex of my thighs.

"What are you doing?" I whisper, reaching for the button on his jeans. "I think it's your turn."

"I might have had an ulterior motive for buying this for you."

"What's that?" My breath catches as he brushes it lightly over my clit before returning it to my thighs. I part my legs instinctively.

"I want to fuck you with this, Hanna. If I can't have my cock inside you, I still want to fuck you."

I slide my hands into his hair and lock my eyes on his. "If you want me, I'm yours. I've told you that."

His kiss is hard and sweet at the same time. I know he's trying to be noble, and I don't want him to be. I release him from his jeans, and he groans as I take his hard length into my hands.

"I'm ready," I promise.

He buries his face in my neck and presses the vibrator lightly against my entrance. The sensation is new and intense, and I cry out even as I rock my hips toward the intrusion.

"Just imagine it's my cock sliding into you."

I want to make a joke about his magically vibrating appendage, but the words die on my lips. I'm too distracted by the round tip of the vibrator poised at my entrance. He slides it in, inch by inch, while kissing my neck. Slowly in. Slowly out. Long, languid movements that already have my body pulsing in response.

"Nate." I try to draw back, to escape the sensation before I'm lost in it. He lowers his mouth to my breast and sucks hard. Then instead of pulling away, I'm rocking forward. Instead of withdrawing from the pleasure, I'm running toward it.

"I can't stop thinking about how it would feel to be inside you," he whispers. "You are so fucking responsive, and I could get off right here just imagining that pussy squeezing around my cock."

I cry out, my hips rising off the bed. "Please."

He groans in my ear and rocks the toy inside me, moving it deeper this time. "I know, baby. I want it as much as you do. But you've done something to me." He removes the vibrator, and I cry out, hungry, empty, desperate.

"Fuck me, Nate." I wouldn't have had the courage to say those words to anyone before meeting him, but he brings out this bold side of me. This wicked side. "Don't make me wait anymore."

"It would be so damn good." He touches the vibrator to my clit and my body squeezes tight, climbing higher. "I'd never get enough of you. I'd fuck you from behind. I'd fuck you with your legs wrapped around my waist. I'd fuck you in the shower and until you thought you couldn't come again."

"Now. Please."

He slides two fingers inside me and holds the vibrator snug

against my clit. "Not until you've made a decision. Not while his ring is waiting in your jewelry box." With those words, he rocks against my clit and curls his fingers, and I'm gone. Flying. Falling. Releasing.

Chapter
SIXTEEN

When my alarm beeps at four thirty on Friday morning, I roll over in bed and bury my face in the pillow, howling in frustration. I thought about Nate Crane all night—his eyes on me, his dirty words, his wicked touch. And when I managed to fall asleep, I dreamed about him.

My body is a live wire of hot need at the memory, an ache pulsing between my legs that I don't want to ignore. For thirty seconds, I lie there with my eyes closed and contemplate sliding my hand beneath the sheets to banish the ache, but guilt has me climbing out of bed.

I take a cool shower before dressing and heading for the bakery, where I lose myself in the comforting motions of baking.

Liz comes in at six and works the front while I experiment with a new cupcake recipe—stress management for bakers.

When Drew comes in after school, Liz hands over front-counter duties and drags me away from my flour and sugar. "Time to stop stewing and get cleaned up."

"What? Who said I'm stewing?" I let her lead me up to my apartment, and I unlock the door for us and push inside.

"You are, aren't you?"

My shoulders sag. "Totally."

"Want to share?"

"I had a Nate Crane memory."

She frowns. "Was it bad?"

I chew on my lower lip and shake my head. "No. It was good. Really good. And now I'm having memory guilt."

We sit in silence for a minute before Liz asks, "Does it bother you not knowing what made you choose Max?"

The question makes me uncomfortable in my own skin. I want to say no. To swear that I don't *need* to know. To say that every morning when I wake up, my heart chooses Max.

But that's not true. My heart? It doesn't know what it wants.

"You don't have to answer that," she whispers.

I sigh. "Bridesmaid dress fitting this afternoon?"

"Yeah. Yours is going to need to be taken in. We ordered them a couple months ago. I think we're going to choose bridesmaid dresses for your wedding while we're there."

"Oh. Yeah, I guess we need to do that."

She frowns. "Don't get too excited."

"What do you mean it doesn't fit?" my mom screeches from the other side of the dressing room door. "That dress fit you perfectly the day we bought it!"

The seamstress studies her shoes and shifts uncomfortably. "I could try the zipper again," she whispers.

I shake my head. "It's no use."

We met Cally, Maggie, and Nix at Cleanstein's to try on our bridesmaid dresses and see if they needed alterations. They pinned mine to be taken in. Then Mom showed up and decided that I should try on my wedding gown for the girls.

"Okay," Mom says, pushing into the dressing room. "We can put off final alterations for, what, another couple of weeks if we need to. You can get the weight back off, can't you, sweetie?"

I look to the seamstress. "Is it possible to take it out?"

"We have maybe half an inch to work with," the seamstress

says. "It might just be enough, but in a dress this style, there's not much wiggle room."

"Let's wait," Mom says. "Hanna's going to fit into it, and if not, we'll take it out." She forces a smile and pats me on the shoulder awkwardly before leaving the dressing room.

The seamstress helps me out of the dress and leaves me alone to study myself in the mirror. Somehow it looks different to me now. The curve of my hips and my breasts. The returning softness of my belly. This is a body two amazing men lose their minds over. It's something beautiful. Something worth caring for.

"Are you okay?" Maggie calls on the other side of the door.

I shake my head to clear it and dress. "I'm fine."

She's waiting outside the door when I exit the dressing room. "I heard it doesn't fit," she whispers.

"I've gained weight." I lower my voice to make sure Mom can't hear. "There are probably only five pounds between me now and me getting that dress zipped, but just staying the size I am now until the wedding is going to be hard enough."

"Would you be offended if I offered my old dress from my canceled wedding?"

I draw in a breath, remembering how much I loved Maggie's dress. She ended up calling off the wedding, and I never thought about what happened to it. "Would it fit me?"

She nods. "It's a ten and it's an A-line, so it's only fitted right above your waist and at your chest. It's in the closet in the guestroom at Asher's if you want to try it on."

"You think Mom would flip out?"

She shrugs. "It's your wedding, Hanna. I think it's more important you wear what *you* want."

Maggie's wedding dress fits like it was made for me.

"Oh, Han-Han," Lizzy breathes. "It's perfect."

The A-line bodice accentuates my breasts while making my waist look small, and the basic bridal satin is covered with the most delicate organza I've ever touched. The satin bodice is heart-shaped, with only the organza continuing over my shoulders in wide, sheer straps.

"Do you want us to stay or do you want to be alone?" Maggie asks as I look at myself in the mirror. "Think about it for a little bit?"

I watch my reflection as I turn side to side. I've never felt so beautiful in my life as I do in this dress. So why does the idea of wearing it in three weeks make me want to weep?

"Can I have a few minutes?"

She nods and ushers Lizzy out of the room with her.

The bedroom has French doors that lead out onto a balcony overlooking the river. I unlock them and pull them open. Desperate for fresh air, I lift my skirt and step out onto the balcony.

I close my eyes as the breeze brushes through my hair. I concentrate on my breathing.

Everything is good. Everything is okay.

My mind scrambles through reassurances, but only one calms me—I don't have to go through with this. If, in a couple weeks, the idea of marriage still panics me, Max would understand. Wouldn't he? Or would I lose him for good? And what would my mom think? She'd be so embarrassed to have another daughter with another botched wedding. Maybe the Thompson girls are cursed.

"Hanna?"

I turn toward the voice to find myself face to face with Nate Crane.

His eyes take me in inch by inch, like he's drinking in what he sees. Me. The dress.

"What are you doing here?" After last night's memory, I'm simultaneously more drawn to him than ever and more wary of being near him. Stepping toward him is as instinctive as breathing, but I catch myself and stop. I clench my hands into fists at my sides. I want to smooth over the hurt between his eyes, to touch his cheek and feel the heat of his skin under my fingertips.

"You look…" His dark eyes scan over me again. "God, you're so beautiful it hurts."

Birds chirp happily and the sun warms my skin, and I hate

myself for wishing I could be seeing him somewhere else. That I could be *someone else.*

"You probably shouldn't be saying things like that to me."

He must hear it, that brokenness in my voice, and he must care something for me, because he lets out this long, shaky breath, as if he's as fucked up over all this as I am. "You're really going to marry him." It's not a question. More like resignation.

I look down to my ring and remember Lizzy's question. *"Does it bother you not knowing what made you choose Max?"*

Nate turns to the river and squeezes the balcony rail until his knuckles go white. "When you told me you had amnesia, I wanted to believe he tricked you into taking that ring."

"Max wouldn't do that."

Nate cuts his gaze to me. There's something in his eyes—a secret locked away—but he doesn't disagree. "For the record, I knew this was how it would end. We both did. It's the amnesia that fucks it all up. Makes this harder than it needs to be."

"Max is perfect for me." I say the words because I don't know what else to say. I need to remind myself that I can't have this man take me into his arms, no matter how desperately I want him to. Not when I chose Max. "And I'm going to tell him the truth. I'm going to tell him that I cheated on him."

His face shifts, that sadness and resignation tightening, hardening into anger. "You didn't *cheat* on Max." He drags a hand through his hair, looking like he wants to throw something. "Jesus. Is that what he made you think?"

"He didn't have to. I remember."

He draws in breath in a sharp hiss. "Everything?"

"Bits. Pieces. Enough to know I was unfaithful."

His jaw ticks, and I can tell he's fighting some kind of internal struggle. Then, as if he can't handle looking at me anymore, he tears his gaze away. "You weren't unfaithful. Not at all. The night you met me—"

"Three months ago. In St. Louis," I supply.

"You remember?" The question is cautiously whispered, but I can't tell if he hopes I do or don't.

I shake my head. "Maggie told me."

"You'd just broken up with Max that night. Come on, Hanna. Use that amazing brain of yours. You aren't the kind of girl who would date one guy and mess around with another. You wouldn't have ever gone out with me that night if you and Max hadn't broken up."

"A breakup?" I almost laugh. "You don't understand small towns. If that were true, everyone would have known."

"But you two didn't want anyone to know. Your mom was helping him get that grant so his business could stay afloat, and you knew she'd stop if you two weren't dating anymore. Things had gotten bad for him—he sold his fucking house, for Christ's sake."

I don't like the logic of those words—the way they dig into my skin and crawl like a hundred parasites.

"You didn't cheat," Nate repeats. "Tell him whatever you want about us, but you weren't unfaithful."

"If we broke up, why wouldn't he have told me?"

"Maybe because he doesn't want you to remember that he broke your heart."

No. "He didn't break anything. He *loves* me. He's good to me. Better than I deserve."

He backs away. One step. Two. The invisible cords connecting us stretch and groan with every inch.

The feeling scares me so much, I lash out. "If you really love me, you'll do something for me."

He laughs, an empty, hollow sound. "You want a favor now?"

"I want you to leave town." It's not a fair request. He hasn't done anything to make me think he's going to disrupt my picture-perfect life. But I fear I'll do something disastrous if I keep running into him. "I want you out of my life." I pray that saying the words might make them true. They're the right words to say—I know that—but they hurt, like someone taking a dull blade to an exposed wound.

"As you wish, angel."

Angel. "Why do you keep calling me that?"

Silence pulses between us for a beat. A living thing. "Because you saved me."

Then I don't have to walk away. He leaves before I can process his words. And I'm grateful. I'm not sure I'm strong enough to walk away from Nate Crane while knowing I'll never see him again.

"Where are you tonight?" Liz asks, waving a hand in front of my face.

I take a deep breath and shake my head. "Sorry. I'm distracted."

We're at a club in Indianapolis—one of those honky-tonk places where they get female customers to dance on the bar. Maggie, Nix, and Cally are on the dance floor while Liz and I watch our drinks at the table.

Liz frowns at me. "Don't pull away from me again, okay? You can talk to me."

"Did Max and I break up before my accident?" I blurt.

She scoots closer. "I'm sorry," she calls over the music. "I thought you asked if you and Max broke up."

I nod. "Did we?"

She frowns. "Not that I know of. Why would you think that?"

"I've been feeling so guilty about Nate, but what if I don't need to feel guilty? What if I was only with Nate after Max and I broke up?"

She shakes her head. "Wouldn't people have known? And then there's the ring. Didn't Max say he proposed *months* ago?"

It's crazy to have this conversation here, in this bar that is so loud I practically have to scream my secrets to the world. But I've held on to Nate's words for over twenty-four hours now and suddenly I can't handle it anymore. I need answers.

"I saw Nate at Maggie's last night, and he said I never cheated on Max. He said Max and I were secretly broken up, and I didn't tell anyone because I didn't want Mom to find out. She was helping him get a grant—a grant that was going to keep his club open."

"The Healthy Tomorrow Grant," Liz says. She swallows hard. "They'll announce the recipient next week, but I'm pretty sure Max is going to get it."

I know this already, yet hearing Liz say it makes my stomach churn.

"Why did you break up?" Liz asks. "And why didn't Max tell you?"

I stare at my drink, Nate's words echoing in my ears. *"Maybe because he doesn't want you to remember that he broke your heart."*

Liz narrows her eyes. "What are you not telling me?"

I exhale a long breath full of worry and second guesses. "What if I'm not the only one in this relationship who hasn't been completely honest?"

"What did he do?"

I tell her about the random text message Max received the night of the engagement party and Max leaving because Meredith needed him. "It's not that I don't believe that's possible. We all know she thinks the world is her freaking oyster, but why is anything she needs more important than being with me? There was something about it that made me feel..."

"Like he was lying," Liz supplies.

Tears fill my eyes as I nod. "I know it's not fair. He's a good guy, and I'm sure I'm just projecting my own guilt onto him or whatever."

She opens her mouth then closes it again before reaching over and taking my hand. "We'll figure this out," she whispers.

"It might not matter anyway. Tomorrow I'm telling him the truth about Nate. If Nate's wrong and Max and I weren't broken up, that might be the end of us anyway."

"He loves you," she assures me.

"Would you want me to marry him if things were the other way around?"

She doesn't answer. She doesn't have to.

I look down at my phone and see the notification light blinking at me. I have a voicemail. "I missed a call. I'm going to go outside and listen to this message."

I wedge my way through the crowd to make it out the front door of the club. My ears breathe a sigh of relief when the door floats closed behind me and takes the noise with it.

"Hanna Cakes!" the woman on my voicemail chirps. "It's Elle! I was hoping I'd catch you in person, but apparently I didn't. Tonight is Cally's bachelorette party, isn't it?"

I frown at the phone because I have no idea who Elle is or why she'd know about the bachelorette party.

She sighs heavily. "Well, I hope you're having a freaking fabulous time because you deserve it. Listen, I'm sorry to throw this at you tonight of all nights. I know you have your own shit you're dealing with right now, but Nate's a freaking mess since he got home last night. He's spiraling out bad. I tried to get him to snap out of it before I left, but he doesn't listen to me. You're the only person who can get through to him. Please go to the house and see what you can do. I don't like to imagine him leaving for his trip in this condition. I'm about to board my plane and then I'm en route to India, and I'll check in when I get there, but then I'll be MIA for a few weeks. Remember that spiritual cleansing I told you about? The one Madonna raves about? Well, they gave me a spot, though the timing is shitty because electronics are a total no-no through the program. Go take care of him, okay?"

I'm still frowning at my phone when Lizzy, Cally, Maggie, and Nix push out of the club, all smiles and excitement.

"Who was it?" Liz asks.

I shake my head. "Nothing important. What's up next?"

"We're going to crash the boys' party at the strip club," Maggie says with a grin.

Nix sidles up beside me. Her request for tonight was that we make her "look like a girl," and when we put her in fitted jeans and a fitted shirt, she said, "No, a slutty girl." So she's wearing a tight black skirt that shows her long, toned legs—apparently I'm not the only runner in this group—and a strapless pink top that shows off her shoulders. She wanted to wear sky-high heels, but we nixed that plan when we saw she wasn't able to walk in them without falling over.

"My nurse called me yesterday afternoon," she says as we move down the sidewalk toward the strip club where the guys are supposed to be. "Your blood work results are back. I'm sorry I haven't been in the office to look at them yet, but I'll be there tomorrow. I'll give you a call."

"I think they took enough blood to give a someone a life-saving infusion," I inform her.

"Sorry about that. I wanted to do the whole workup again."

"Don't go into the office just for that. It's fine. I'm eating."

I take a deep breath of the cool night air and think about that voicemail. I scan my memory again and again, but I can't remember an Elle. Obviously it's someone I know from Nate's life.

"Have you told Max yet?" Nix asks quietly.

"Tomorrow. That's the plan." I wanted him to be able to enjoy Will's bachelor party without my nasty secret hanging over him.

"Huh. Maybe we should work out some sort of Bat Signal so I can interrupt with the blood work call if it's not going well."

"There it is!" Liz calls, pointing to the building in front of us.

There's a long line out front, but the bouncer waves us over.

"Does he know we're coming?" I ask Liz.

She snorts. "No, but we're a group of five hot-ass girls going into a gentleman's club. We probably won't have to pay for a drink all night."

I laugh, but my moment of good humor is cut off when a familiar voice calls, "Oh, look who's there."

When my eyes land on Meredith coming out of the club, I want to puke. She might have just had a baby a few months ago, but she's as gorgeous as ever in a tiny black dress and heels, her long, silky blond hair hanging past her bare shoulders.

"What are you doing here?" I sneer.

She leans against the building and crosses her feet at her ankles. "Oh, nothing special. Just hanging with some…friends. I hear you lost your memory."

"What's it to you?" It's not just a smartass retort. I want to know.

She shrugs. "I was out of town when it happened so I just heard. Me and baby girl got back last weekend. But I guess you know that since Max came to help me out for a while. He's such a natural with kids."

She winks at me like we share a secret, and I want to slap her.

Meredith's eyes rake over Cally in her bride-to-be shirt. "What's up, Cally? Are you here to pick up your check?"

Cally's hands clench and her jaw ticks but she doesn't respond.

Meredith's glossed lips curl into an ugly smile. "Quite a step up from your...previous employment."

Cally seethes beside me, and Liz steps forward. "Don't you have a baby you should be home caring for?"

Meredith rolls her eyes. "That's what babysitters are for."

"You ladies coming in?" the bouncer asks.

"Have fun," Meredith calls. "I know I did."

I follow the girls into the club, but the energy of our whole group has changed. None of us are in the mood to party anymore. Instead, we all want to know what Meredith was doing here and if it had anything to do with our guys.

And that's just what she intended.

"I hate her," Lizzy spits.

Cally squeezes her shoulder. "Let it go. She's petty and shallow and not worth our energy."

Maggie forces a smile. "Come on. The guys reserved the room in the back."

We follow her through the tables and past the stage to a private party room with its own bar. Will and Max are together at the back of the room filled with a dozen or so other guys I don't know.

"Damn, looking good, Hanna," Sam says when he spots me. He's almost vertical, though remaining upright appears to be a struggle, and he smells like a bottle of scotch.

"Thank you, Sam."

He winks at Liz. "You too, I guess."

"Gee, thanks," Liz drones. "I'm just wondering what Meredith was doing here."

Sam shrugs. "She just wanted to hang for a while. But watch out, Hanna," he says, raising his drink. "She's apparently given up on Will and set her sights on your man. She could hardly keep her hands off him tonight."

"Hanna," Liz whispers, but I'm already rushing away from them, hurrying toward Max before my fear of the truth trumps my need to know.

Max does a double take when he sees me. "What are you doing here?"

I hold out my hand. "Give me your phone." I'm not sure what's shaking more, my hand or my voice.

His smile falters. "What's wrong? Did something happen to Cally?"

A wave of nausea hits me hard, and I slide my hand into his pocket and retrieve the phone myself.

"Hanna, stop." His voice is hard, but before he can take it from me, Lizzy's there, pushing him back.

"What's going on?" Will asks. Then he sees Cally and grins. "My night just got a hell of a lot better."

I swipe my finger over the screen to unlock it, and Max whispers, "Can we talk about this?"

But it's too late. I've already pulled up the texts on his phone and found the messages that came after our engagement party.

Meredith: I need a favor. Can you be here in ten?

Meredith: Fuck you, Max. I'm losing my mind. She's your baby too. Come over here and give me a fucking break.

I lift my head, and Max looks so damn forlorn I'd feel sorry for him if it weren't for this terrible ache in my chest. "Is this a joke?" My whole world is this elaborately woven tapestry, and he's holding the single loose strand. If he tugs, it will unravel. If he pulls just right, it will all fall apart.

Liz takes the phone from my hands and reads. "Holy baby mama drama."

"But...she bought sperm, right?" I gulp in air and remind myself to breathe. "She was artificially inseminated."

Max looks to Will, who's holding Cally in his arms. Will looks confused. He can join the fucking club.

"I'm sorry, brother," Max says. "You weren't serious about her and you know I've always been hung up on Meredith. Like an idiot. But I swear I didn't sleep with her until after Cally came back."

Will's chest rises and falls and his jaw hardens. "Man, you're apologizing to the wrong person."

Max's gaze shifts back to me and he shakes his head. "I didn't know the baby was mine. I...suspected, maybe? But she said she'd been artificially inseminated. She didn't tell me the baby was mine until weeks after she was born."

"When was that?" I whisper.

"About three months ago."

My heart hurts.

Lizzy smacks Max in the chest. "And when were you going to tell Hanna, huh?"

"She already knew." He swallows but doesn't take his eyes off me. "I just hadn't told her *again* yet." He drops his voice. "I didn't know how. Say something, Hanna."

"I'm sorry," I whisper. "But I think I need to leave."

Chapter
SEVENTEEN

" I NEED A flight to LA, please."
The woman behind the counter at the Southwest Airlines desk takes my ID and credit card and clicks at her keyboard.

My phone buzzes in my hand.

Liz: What do you mean you're GOING TO LA?

Some mornings, I wake up with new memories. Usually, they're nothing important.

"I can get you on a one o'clock flight out," the woman says, quoting me a dollar figure that would send my rational self running in the other direction. But I'm not feeling terribly rational today.

"Sounds perfect. Put it on the card."

I went to sleep last night knowing I could forgive Max for his omission. I understood why it would have been hard to tell me about the baby. I could see that. And it hurt. But I closed my eyes, planning to talk to him today, to forgive him for his omission and make things right by telling him what I know about my relationship with Nate.

"Any bags to check?" she asks.

"Nope."

I went to bed feeling spent and hurt but hopeful. We were going to get through this.

She returns my cards and hands me a boarding pass. "Have a nice flight."

"Thank you."

I head for security and my phone buzzes again.

Liz: Max just called me wanting to know if I know where you are. He was really upset. What the hell is going on?

Some mornings, I wake up with new memories. Once, I woke up with the memory of Max flirting with me at Brady's, my cheeks burning as I realized maybe he was sincere in his attraction to me.

The Indianapolis airport is quiet this morning, and the blue-shirted guy at security checks my boarding pass and ID. "Los Angeles, huh? Business or pleasure?"

"A little of both, I guess." I force a smile. Because that's what I do. I smile to make people comfortable. I smile when my heart hurts, and I act like everything's okay when I've been betrayed.

"Think you'll see any stars while you're there?" the next guy asks while I take off my shoes.

"I'm almost sure of it." I plop my carry-on, purse, and cell onto the conveyor belt next to my shoes and inch through the metal detector.

Some mornings, I wake up with new memories. A couple of days ago, I went to bed without a single memory of my opening day at the bakery, and when my alarm went off the next morning, I could recall the terror of my first day with a new business like it was yesterday.

"Thanks, ma'am," calls the lady behind the metal detector screen. "Have a nice flight."

Nodding, I grab my shoes and bag. I'm reaching for my phone when it starts to ring. Lizzy's face flashes on the screen, though I didn't need to see her picture to know it was her.

I put it to my ear. "Hello."

"Talk to me."

"I'm going to LA."

"And you told your fiancé you couldn't marry him. What the hell did I miss?"

I scan the signs and turn right to head toward my terminal. "I need to see him."

"Did you have a new memory? Hanna, come on."

"I can't talk about it right now. I understand if you need to close the bakery while I'm gone. You've already done more than I should ever have asked."

"I'll run the bakery. That's not a problem." The line goes quiet, and I know she's picking up on how serious I am about being unable to talk. We're twins, after all. We have that connection. And now, more than ever, I'm glad it's back. Because I really can't do this. I can't talk right now. I'll lose it. "If you want me to come out there with you, you just say the word."

"Thank you." My voice glitches over the words like a scratch on a record. "I'll text you when I land."

"I love you."

"Love you too," I whisper. And I end the call, loneliness tearing at my chest.

Some mornings, I wake up with new memories. Usually, they're nothing. This morning when I woke up, I remembered the night three months ago when I ended my relationship with Max because he had broken my heart.

May—Three Months Before Accident

"God, I'm so jealous of you I could spit." Lizzy grabs Cally's hand and holds it in front of her to inspect her ring. It's girls' night at Brady's and the table is full of empty glasses and half-full margarita pitchers.

"I'm the luckiest," Cally says, grinning.

Lizzy snorts. "Pretty, lucky, and gracious. Almost makes you hate her. So did you have to train the muscles in that arm to keep that rock on there all the time?"

"Shut up! It's not that big!"

My phone buzzes in my purse, alerting me to a new text message. I grin, immediately thinking it's from Max. He wanted to see me tonight but didn't push when he found out the girls were getting together for margaritas.

I pull my phone out and open my text messages. I frown at the screen. I don't recognize the number.

Unknown Number: *When are you going to give it up? Max is way out of your league.*

My stomach pitches into my chest and drags my heart with it as it falls back down. The words are not only cruel, they're exactly what I fear. I've wanted Max since we were teenagers, and now that I have him, sometimes it feels too good to be true.

I'm still trying to decide whether to text back when another beeps through.

Unknown Number: *You can keep fooling yourself if you want, but while he's dating your fat ass, he's wishing he were with someone he's actually attracted to.*

"Hanna?" Lizzy says. "Is everything okay?"

I paste on a smile to cover the sick churning of my stomach. I could tell the girls about these messages, bask in the reassuring warmth of their righteous indignation. We could talk about lying, jealous bitches who will go to any length to drag happy people into their misery. The conversation would no doubt end in all of us laughing and me deciding to ignore this nastiness.

But what if the person on the other end of this text conversation is telling the truth?

"Yeah. I'm fine." I text back. I shouldn't engage. I should find out who these are coming from and show them to my friends, to Max.

Hanna: *Who is this?*
Unknown Number: *This is the sexy bitch your boyfriend wishes he were fucking.*

"I'll be right back," I say in a rush. It's not so much the text as the series of screenshots attached to it that has me shaking. I have to get away from this table before the tears come. I can't let the girls see.

I barely make it to the bathroom before I start crying, and Meredith is waiting on the other side of the door, a smirk on her face.

"Why so sad, Hanna?"

I stumble back. "You?"

She smiles prettily and touches up her perfect lipstick in the mirror. "I didn't think I wanted him," she says. "I mean, I'm more interested in a man who can really support me, you know. But then things didn't work out with William because apparently he has a thing for whores—"

"Don't!" I growl, my nails biting into my palms.

"You're all so cute. Sticking up for each other. Why don't you go get your friends? I can show them my old texts too. We'll see what they think about your perfect boyfriend then."

"Why do you even care about this? Didn't you just have a baby?"

"I did. Which is why I've decided it's time to be proactive."

"What do you want from me?"

"Max," she says simply. "I want what you have, and as you might have noticed from those messages, he wants me."

"Then why is he with me?" I force myself to ask. Because that's the only defense I have. Meredith is beautiful. She's thin and blond and perfect. Everything I'll never be. And the texts between her and Max are so damning that I want to wilt like an unwatered flower in the hot sun.

"Come on, Hanna. Everyone knows your family is loaded. Max's little health club isn't going to get him very far if he doesn't have a sugar mama to bail him out."

I open my mouth to defend him then close it. Because it's true. I've already called in a favor with my mom and her friends to try to get Max a grant to help him pay the mortgage on his club. And I can tell by the Cheshire Cat grin on Meredith's face that she knows that too.

"I'm done waiting, Hanna, and he needs your money too much to leave you. So…" She shrugs. "I figured it was time to let you in on our little secret so you could hurry things along my way."

It feels like there's a rabid animal frantically clawing its way out of my stomach. I can't look at her anymore. I can't stand here and listen to her.

I turn around and grab the door handle, but her words stop me.

"Oh, I copied Max on that last one. I couldn't risk you pretending you never saw it just so you could keep him. Now you can pretend if you want, but you'll both know and things will never be the same between you."

I don't look at her before pushing through the door and leaving the bathroom.

"I've gotta get going," I say when I reach the table.

Lizzy frowns at me. "Why? What happened? Who were those texts from?"

My twin knows me too well, but I paste on a smile and shake my head. "I'm just not feeling very well. I'll see you at home later."

I don't wait for their permission or even their goodbyes, and I head out the door and toward home. I've had too much alcohol tonight to drive, so I walk the half-mile through town to my rental house, my heels pinching my feet painfully with every step.

Max is waiting at the door when I get there, his face drawn with worry. "It's not what it looks like."

I nod and step into his foyer. "Good." My voice is clear and strong, and some distant part of my mind is just proud that I'm not collapsing in a pathetic heap at his feet, begging him to love me, pleading with him to explain this away. "Because it looks like you're a lying asshole."

He drags a hand through his hair. "Hanna, don't. Okay? You weren't supposed to see those texts."

"Oh my God. Seriously? That's the best you've got? I wasn't supposed to *see* that our relationship is a total sham? That it's *pretend*? That you—" A sob rips through my chest before I can finish. It hurts too much.

"But it's not," he growls. I try to step around him, but he grabs my hand and holds it tight. "This is real. Nothing about what I feel for you is pretend."

"But it was. At one point it *was*."

"I was an idiot," he whispers. "Such an idiot."

"You don't understand what it's like to feel like shit about the way you look. You don't understand what a leap of faith it was for me to believe you wanted to be with me when you could have had any woman you wanted in this town."

"Meredith and I have a long, screwed-up history, and until things were serious with Will and Cally—"

"Leave." I point to the door.

"Don't do this, Hanna. Those texts were from *December*. That was months ago. You and I hadn't even kissed yet. I had no idea I was going to fall in love with you."

"Stop. I can't do this." I shake my head. "I have spent too many years of my life hating myself. I can't be with you anymore. I can't..." I shrug and tears spill onto my cheeks. "Please leave."

"I'll give you time, but please—"

"It's over, Max. Leave." I sound wild. Crazed. Maybe I am.

When he walks out the door, I sink to the floor and wrap my arms around my knees as I sob. I don't need to look at my phone again to remember the texts. They're branded on my brain.

Meredith: You're seriously going out with Hanna Fat Ass Thompson.

Max: You're seriously going to start this conversation by being a bitch?

Meredith: Just tell me how this happened.

Max: It's a temporary arrangement. She needs a self-esteem boost.

Meredith: I had no idea you were taking charity cases.

Max: No worries, I still prefer blondes.

Meredith: So what's it like to fuck a fatty?

Max: Don't be a bitch.

Meredith: He dodges the question.

Max: Trust me, I'm not going to let this charade go that far. She's a sweet girl, but she's not my type.

Meredith: Am I your type?

Max: You know you are. But last I checked you were still hung up on Will Bailey.

Meredith: That was so last month. Come over here and I'll prove it.

Max: What do you have in mind?

Meredith: You. My mouth. More specifically, your dick and my mouth.

Max: Shit. Don't say that when you know I can't.

Meredith: You said yourself that your thing with Hanna is just a charade.

Max: I don't want her hurt. Period. I'll have to take a rain check.

Meredith: I can keep a secret. I know when to use my mouth. And where.

Max: This is a bad idea.

Meredith: I'll see you in fifteen, then?

Max: Make that five.

Chapter
EIGHTEEN

WHEN I climb into a cab at the airport and say, "Nate Crane's house, please," I almost expect the guy to laugh at me. Instead, he shakes his head, mutters something about tourists, and starts the drive to Hollywood Hills.

"Nate Crane lives right past those gates," he announces in a bored tone.

The house in question is lit up like Granny's last birthday cake, and the circle drive has so many high-end cars that it would make the nicest (er, *only*) dealer in New Hope weep.

"Where ya wanna go next? Eminem's home isn't far from here."

"No. This is where I'll get out, thanks."

"You know they don't just let you come party with 'em, right?"

I smile and hand him cash for my fare. He looks at me like I've lost my mind but shrugs as I climb out of the back.

When I walk up to the gate, there are two security guards in black suits. Big guys.

"Sorry, ma'am," a dark-skinned man calls from in front of the gate. "Private party."

"Keep walking," his white comrade instructs.

"Yeah, um." *Shit.* I didn't really prepare to face the Men in Black to get to Nate. "I—"

"Jesus, Hanna, girl? Is that you?" The first guy slides his sunglasses down his nose and peers at me over the tops. "What are you wearing?" He nods to one of the other guys then grabs me by the upper arm as the gates slide open.

So I guess I'm going to get in after all, because next thing I know, he's sitting me in a golf cart and driving me up to the house. Without a word, he leads me out, up the front stairs, and into the house.

"Nate lives here?" The massive marble staircase fills the entryway with all the pomp and circumstance of a grand museum. Crystal chandeliers hang overhead. Somehow, it doesn't seem fitting of the secretly dorky rocker I know so little about.

The man frowns at me. "What's wrong with you?" He shakes his head. "I can't have you going back there dressed like this. Not with all those hos hanging around."

It's my turn to frown. I wasn't exactly worried about my ensemble of a T-shirt and jeans when I left my house this morning. I was more worried about getting the hell out of Dodge. Anyway, I'm not here to compete with any "hos." I just want a chance to talk to Nate.

"Um, do we know each other?" I ask the man as we head up the stairs.

He leads me into an impressive, large bedroom with an even more impressive walk-in closet. "Oh, you think you're funny and you're going to act like you don't know me, huh? Well, play coy all you want, but those girls Crane has over tonight aren't playing games."

"What are—" I'm cut off by my own shriek as the man yanks my ponytail holder from my hair and my T-shirt off over my head.

I wrap my arms around myself, trying for what modesty I can.

He wriggles his eyebrows. "Well, at least you wore the good underwear." Then he's scanning the closet and I relax. This man isn't interested in ogling me. In fact, if I had to guess… "Damn good thing you have a gay man around to dress you tonight, sweetheart. Because them bitches out back aren't messing around."

I gasp dramatically. "You're telling me there are both bitches *and* hos here tonight?"

"You think you're cute," he says, moving his head side to side, "but they're 'bout to steal your man."

"He's not my man."

The man rolls his eyes and waves away my objection. "This!" He pulls a bright red dress from the rack and offers it to me.

"Whose clothes are these?"

"Well, they're Janelle's, of course. Now get changed and walk by that boy before he does something he regrets. I don't know what you did to him, but he's been in a bad way since he got back here Friday night. Drinking, partying. Hiding from something." He raises an eyebrow and gives me an unimpressed once-over. "You know what you did."

"Actually, I—"

"Change. Then meet Jamaal in the bathroom to freshen that makeup."

He's halfway out of the closet when I ask, "Who's Jamaal?" It's only one question of the approximately 1700 that are floating around in my mind right now, but since I'm supposed to see "Jamaal" next, I guess it takes priority.

The man stops, turns, and glares at me. "I thought you were clean, girl? You know that's why Janelle liked you. None of the drugs and bullshit. Now get changed and meet me in the bathroom."

"Jamaal!" I hold my breath. Could this flamboyant man be such a walking cliché that he speaks of himself in the third person?

The man stops and turns. "Yes, princess?"

I grin. I can't help it. I like this guy. A lot. "I don't remember you."

He snorts. "Don't be a bitch. Nobody forgets Jamaal."

"No, I…" I shake my head and bite back my laughter. "I don't remember much of anything from the last year. I had a head injury, and I have amnesia."

His big brown eyes grow impossibly wider. "No shit?"

"No shit," I say solemnly. "And the more I find out about what I've forgotten…" I swallow, struggling to verbalize the strange but undeniable impulse that brought me here. "The more I learn, the more I realize I need to spend time with Nate before shutting him out of my life."

"Why would you shut him out? That's crazy talk," he says. I hold up my left hand, and Jamaal draws in a long breath, his nostrils flaring as he presses his hand to his chest. "Who gave you *that* pathetic excuse for a jewel?"

"Does the name Max Hallowell ring any bells?"

He shakes his head and makes a tsking sound. "You don't remember Nathaniel? Truly?"

Nathaniel. I like that. Fits with the comic book T-shirts and Hulk tattoo. *Nathaniel.* "When I woke up in the hospital, I didn't remember him at all. Now I only remember bits and pieces. I just want him to talk to me."

He hums, noncommittal. "Change and meet me in the bathroom." With a flourish, he shuts the doors behind him and leaves me alone in the brightly lit closet.

I like Jamaal enough that I decide to follow his directions rather than questioning him. I strip out of my clothes and pull the red dress overhead. It's too small for me, but he chose a dress that stretches nicely, and after a bit of yanking and tugging, it covers my hips almost respectably. I spot a pair of matching red heels on the shoe rack and grin when I see that they're my size. I might feel uncomfortable in this dress, but I love shoes. I've always loved shoes. Shoes always fit.

My phone buzzes in my purse and I pull it out to see a new text.

Nix: *You need to call me. STAT.*

I don't want to talk to anyone from home right now. I can't handle the sympathy I know they want to deliver.

When I exit the closet, I don't have a chance to look for the bathroom before Jamaal is whistling at me—à la calling Fido, not à la catcall—and waving me into another room.

I gasp as I step into the glitzy bathroom. *Glitz* is the only word for it. Marble and glass, mirrors and crystal. It's a large, shining space that's too over the top to belong on anything but an episode of *Cribs.*

"If you're going to stand there with your mouth hanging open, at least turn to me so I can touch you up while you gawk."

I obey, and Jamaal's large hands begin applying mascara, blush, and lip gloss in a rather expert way. When he's done, I can only blink at myself in the mirror. In less than three minutes, he managed to transform me from Plain Jane to one of the LA-caliber women I saw milling at the airport.

"Wow."

"You're welcome. Now let's hurry down to the pool and find that fool man of yours before he does something really stupid."

"He's not my man, Jamaal."

He snorts in reply and leads me back out into the hallway, but instead of taking the stairs that brought us up here, he leads me to the back of the hall and opens a door to a small, narrow set of stairs.

"Be careful in those heels." When we hit the bottom, Jamaal points the way toward the back door. "There you go, kiddo. He's out there making an ass of himself."

I study the large French doors and the scantily clad women beyond. Some of them are dressed like I am now, in dresses and heels. Others are in bikinis and sarongs. Others still in bikinis and heels. Because bitches and hos, I guess.

They're *all* painted and more beautiful than I will ever be without surgical enhancement. Knowing I'm going to step out there like I'm one of them makes my stomach cramp painfully.

"You've got something none of those women have," Jamaal says from behind me, as if reading my thoughts.

"What's that?"

"A mind of your own, kid. Why do you think he likes you so much?" He tilts up my chin and studies my face in the light. "You really don't remember? That's not just a bunch of bullshit?"

"I really don't. Did I come here a lot?"

He shrugs. "A couple of times."

My gaze drifts back toward the door and the music trickling in from outside. Someone screeches, and I hear a splash.

"What am I going to do if he won't talk to me?"

Jamaal shrugs. "Janelle will call. We'll get her to help. He can't say no to her."

Right. Janelle. The woman whose clothes I'm wearing. "And who's Janelle?"

"Janelle Crane? How hard did you hit that head?"

He walks away as the name clicks into place in my mind. *Janelle Crane.* The actress. I struggle to keep my jaw hinged as I look down at my dress. I'm wearing Janelle Crane's dress. Janelle Crane's shoes. *Holy. Shit.*

"Martini?"

I jump at the voice. A woman is standing next to me with a tray of martini glasses filled with light pink liquid. "Um, no thanks."

She smiles politely and heads out the door.

Rolling my shoulders back and lifting my chin, I follow her.

The back of the house is as gorgeous as the front. A large pool sits off to the right, surrounded by several tables and countless loungers. The space is overwhelmed with people, mostly women, and pounding music fills my ears. Women dance against each other, drink, and splash in the pool. And at least three look at me like I have two heads and should leave immediately.

I lift my chin and scan the scene for Nate. The only man in a crowd of women shouldn't be that hard to find.

I spot him in the hot tub, using his mouth to take a shot glass from between a woman's breasts. I stamp down the jealousy I feel at the sight and want to kick the shit out of myself.

My ego was battered and beaten by my memory of what Max did. Naturally, I thought I'd make myself feel better by visiting a celebrity who buries his face in the tits of whatever woman is handy. This was a stellar plan. Yet I can't turn around. I keep moving, keep heading toward Nate and this I-don't-know-what I'm after.

The click of my heels against the stone patio is muffled by the music and chatter, but I narrow in on the sound, concentrate on it as I cross to him.

He's laughing about something, but when his gaze settles on me, his smile falls away. And after the way I treated him last time I saw him, who can blame him?

"Well, look who came to party," he says, his words only slightly slurred.

He's drunk. I can see it in his eyes. Hell, I can practically smell the booze rolling off everyone in that hot tub.

"Can we talk?" My words come out meek, and I wish I could take them back and replace them with a command. *We need to talk.* Something. Anything other than sounding and feeling weak and unwanted. I'm so sick of feeling unwanted.

"What do you think, ladies?" he asks the woman around him. "Is there room for one more?"

The women pout and crowd around Nate. "Aren't we enough for you, Crane?" one asks. Another says, "Things were just getting interesting." And another complains, "It's already crowded in here. There's hardly room for *her*."

The jab at my size hurts worse than it would have fifty pounds ago. Because in my size tens, I'm bigger than the rest of them, the kind of women who scour racks for extra-small shorts. It hurts more than it would have before because this is as good as I get and I know it. In fact, *this* probably isn't going to last.

I'm so stupid. I have a man at home who loves me. Who is more than I deserve. Who looks at me like I'm his world. Max screwed up. He hurt me. Betrayed me. But I can imagine a life with him, raising our kids in New Hope alongside our friends. So why am I here?

Nate's gaze rakes over me, from my head to my toes, trailing electric fingers of need in its path. Why does my body react when he looks at me like this? "You want to talk?" he says, lifting heavy-lidded eyes back to mine. "Climb on in." He turns to the women around him. "Sorry, ladies. I'm gonna need you to leave for a bit. You're right. No room for her and all of you, and I like her more."

The women whine in unison and fawn at Nate. He locks his eyes on mine for two beats before pressing a hard, open-mouthed kiss to the woman next to him. It's wet, sloppy, and entirely for my benefit, and I won't give him the satisfaction of looking away.

My stomach clenches, but I keep my face impassive as he releases her and the three women climb out of the hot tub, seemingly unconcerned with their bare chests.

He doesn't even watch them go. HeeHe just he leans his head back, closes his eyes, and says, "You wanna talk, you're gonna have to climb in."

"I'm—" I shake my head, which is stupid since he can't see me. "I'm not wearing a swimsuit."

He lifts his head, and this time his gaze lands on my left hand. "I guess it can wait, then."

"I came all the way here," I say in a hard whisper. I don't want to call too much attention to myself. "The least you can do is talk to me."

"A lot of people visit me here." He picks up a shot glass off the back of the tub and throws it back. "Too bad you didn't bring a suit. We could have that talk you're so set on."

Fuck it. Even in underwear and a bra, I'll be more modestly covered than most of the women here tonight. I kick off my shoes and peel the dress off over my head. I fold it neatly before setting it in a chair. The last thing I want to do is be responsible for ruining Janelle Crane's dress.

When I turn back to the hot tub, his eyes are on me again, hot and greedy and…something else. There's something more in those eyes this time. Sadness?

"Take the bra off too," he orders as I step in.

"Dream on." I sink into the water and have to swallow back a sigh as it bubbles around me and warms my skin. I've had such a long, shitty day, and I could really use a relaxing soak. Instead, I'll talk to this jackass. Did I actually believe he was the person I needed when my heart was hurting?

He's watching me carefully. "Last time we talked, you made it profoundly clear you didn't want to see me again."

"I changed my mind."

"Yet I don't remember inviting you here."

"You sure know how to make a girl feel welcome. And is this seriously your house? It doesn't seem like you at all."

"Oh, so you know me now? Is that memory back?"

My cheeks burn with my blush. "Some of it."

"Yeah?" He drops his gaze down to my breasts. "Anything good?"

"I remembered that I broke up with Max. I remembered that I never cheated on him. I remembered how much he hurt me."

He sighs and leans his head back on the edge of the tub. "I'm not interested in being some prop for revenge."

"This isn't about revenge."

He doesn't look at me. "Sure it isn't."

"I called off the wedding."

"I'll believe that when his ring's not on your finger. Why are you here, Hanna?"

"I'm here because nothing is as it seemed and…" And what? Why *am* I here? "You said you were in love with me."

"Yeah, well, what was it you said? *We all make mistakes*?"

"Was the mistake being in love with me or telling me that you were?" I don't know why it matters so much that I know, but right now it seems so important that I'd do almost anything to get an honest answer from him.

"What do you want from me?" He sounds almost bored.

I scan the party going on in full swing around us. The women, the booze, the superficial bullshit. "I just want to talk to you. Without all these people. Without all the secrets."

He lifts a brow and grabs a phone from the ledge of the tub. He taps the screen then puts it down, and within seconds, Jamaal is coming out the back door with several other men in black suits.

"Party's over," Jamaal calls. "Thank you for coming. We hope you had a good time. Now it's time to leave. You don't have to go home but you can't stay here."

I blink in amazement as everyone does as he says, and minutes later, Nate and I are alone, the music is off, and the only sound is the whir of the hot tub's jets and the hum of traffic in the distance.

"That better?" he asks softly. And maybe he's not as drunk as I thought. And maybe he's not bored with my presence. His eyes dip to my cleavage and back up, roaming over my face. Again, I get that feeling that he's drinking me in. Memorizing me.

I swallow. The truth is that I want to memorize him too. The hard angles of his cheekbones and jaw, the dark brown of his bedroom eyes, the softness of his beautiful mouth.

"Don't look at me like that," he whispers.

"Why not? Maybe I should have let myself look at you the night you showed up in my bed. Maybe I should have made you talk to me then. Maybe if I knew what *you* know, I'd understand why I chose him instead of you."

He lets out a breath and closes his eyes. I gather every bit of my courage and turn to him, straddling his lap and wrapping my arms behind his neck.

His eyes fly open. "What are you doing?"

"This isn't about revenge."

He brushes my jaw with the back of his knuckles.

I lean into his touch, the gentle reassurance of it. "It's not about Max. It's about us."

Pain slices over his face and he drops his hand. "There is no *us*, Hanna."

"I don't remember making that choice. Just—"

His expression hardens. "There was no *choice*. Not about me. It was never a choice between me and Max. The only choice you had to make was whether to take Max back or not."

"I don't understand."

"I never offered you what he did. The life, the marriage, the commitment. The happily-ever-fucking-after. I can't. I won't. It wasn't a choice between him and me because I wasn't offering you those things."

I wilt and back away from him. If our relationship was purely physical, why do I feel this way? "You and me? This? It was just about sex?"

"Not even at first."

"Then how—" I squeeze my eyes shut as the memory crashes over me and the understanding right along with it.

It was never a choice between two men.

"I'm sorry," he breathes. "You have no idea how sorry." Water sloshes as he stands and climbs out.

I follow numbly, not sure what else I'm supposed to do with myself.

He hands me a towel but doesn't meet my eyes. "Come on. You can sleep in Janelle's room."

Into the house and back up the narrow stairs, he leads me to the room where Jamaal ushered me upon my arrival.

After clicking on a lamp, Nate disappears into the closet and returns with gray cotton pajamas. "These should fit," he says. "You can stay as long as you want. You're always welcome."

I'm still reeling from the memory. "I feel...really stupid."

"Don't." He tilts my chin until I'm looking at him. Then he drops his hand quickly, as if touching me costs him. "Please don't."

Chapter NINETEEN

August—Five Days Before Accident

THE DELICIOUS smells of bacon, cinnamon, and pastry dough wake me.

I roll over and stretch, my body spent in that most delicious way, my muscles singing with happiness. If a weekend in bed doing everything *but* making love makes me feel this good, how good would I feel if Nate would sleep with me?

I don't want to go back to New Hope. I want to stay here in LA in Nate's big-ass house, where life seems less like this ominous dark cloud waiting to be confronted and more like when I played pretend as a kid.

I climb out of bed and head to the bathroom, where I wash my face, brush my teeth, and try to calm the worst of my bed-head. After throwing on a robe, I head down to the kitchen.

Nate stands bare-chested and beautiful behind the island, the muscles in his forearms flexing as his competent hands chop apples and peaches and throw them into a bowl. Behind him, bacon sizzles on the stove, the smell incredible.

My stomach rumbles.

"Looks like you're cooking for an army this morning."

He looks up, noticing me for the first time since I entered the kitchen. His eyes light with his smile. He wipes his hands on a towel and skirts around the island to pull me into his arms and kiss me soundly. When he breaks the kiss and steps back, I have to grab the edge of the counter to keep my balance.

If only this were real life.

"What are you doing with all this food?" I survey the pan of rolls cooling on the counter next to some sort of casserole that looks like it has more cheese than I've let myself eat in months.

"I'm feeding my girl."

My cheeks flush. I'm embarrassed that he thinks I require so much for breakfast. Downside of being a big girl. "I just need some coffee and maybe a little of that fruit salad."

He raises a brow. "What you need is a keeper. How much weight have you lost since we met three months ago?"

Thirty-eight and a half pounds. Add that to the ten I managed to drop the five months prior and I'm almost down fifty pounds. But I know Nate won't like my answer, so I avoid the question and cross to the coffee pot to pour myself a steaming mugful. The creamer sits next to the pot, and I look at it for a minute, tempted. *Empty calories.*

When I turn around, he's right in front of me.

"Hanna," he whispers, tilting my chin up so I'm looking him in the eye. "I'm worried about you."

"I needed to lose some weight. Trust me, I'm not going to waste away."

"You didn't need to lose an ounce." He *is* worried. I can see it in his eyes. "Did he do this to you? Did he make you feel this way?"

No need to say who *he* is. "It doesn't matter."

"Fuck, Hanna. What did this loser do to you?"

"He's not a loser!" I shut my mouth and study my coffee. Max is off-limits, and Nate usually respects that.

"So you haven't given him an answer yet."

I gasp, horrified that it's not obvious. "I wouldn't be here if I had."

Nate gives a sad sort of half-smile and backs up a step. "Yeah, but you see, that assumes you're going to take him back. If you'd answered and told him no, there'd be nothing wrong with being here with me."

He goes back to his breakfast preparations, the silence snapping between us with so many things unsaid.

When breakfast is done, Nate serves both of us. I know I won't eat much of the calorie-laden breakfast—doing so would make me sick at this point—but I don't argue when he fills my plate.

We sit at the glass table in the sunroom, the slow morning rain tapping on the glass. I wish for clear skies and sunshine to warm my skin through the glass. I close my eyes for a minute, imagining it, the hope it normally makes me feel.

"I'm sorry, Hanna," Nate says, and when I open my eyes, he's watching me. "I know you love Max. I just…" His jaw works as he shifts his gaze to something beyond the glass. The bird bathing itself in the garden? Maybe something that can't be seen.

"What do you want me to do?" My voice breaks on the question. I really want him to answer because I don't know what I'm supposed to do. I'm putting us all through this painful holding pattern until I can get my mind straight. I'm just waiting, assuming the answer will come to me. Or am I really waiting for Nate to offer me more than he has?

His fork clatters against his plate and he shakes his head. "Nothing. I'm not asking anything from you. I'm not him."

I close my eyes. It's not fair to want a declaration of love from this man. He was upfront with me from the beginning. He's not about the relationship, not about the forever.

Pushing back from the table, I stand up and head out to the patio. I stand under the awning and watch the rain dance on the water in the pool.

"It's not you." The sound of Nate's voice sends a tremor of sadness through me. Because he's never asked anything from me, but part of me wants him to. "You know that, right?" He stands next to me, head tilted back, eyes on the sky. "I can't offer you more than this. Even when you deserve more. It's not because I don't want it. It's because I made a promise to myself. To my son."

Turning, I run my fingers across the date tattooed above his left pec. He told me the significance of that date the first night we met. It's his son's birthday. The day he says his world changed. "I never asked you for more, Nate."

He grabs my fingers and squeezes them in his. "But you deserve it."

"I'm a big girl. Let me decide what I deserve."

"You deserve everything. Anything you could want." His grip is nearly painful on my fingers, but I don't pull away. I'm too worried he'll stop talking. "But I'm not the man to give that to you. I can't."

You won't, I think.

His eyes scan the dark and angry sky. "My dad left my mom when Janelle and I were eight. It always sucks for kids when their parents split, but he moved out of our house and into Jayda's. She was already pregnant with his baby, and I remember when my stepsister was born. You should have seen my dad's eyes when he looked at her. Like she was the most precious thing he'd ever been given. Then Jayda had a second child, and a third. He was so damn happy with them. For a while, he did his visitation with Janelle and me. We'd go over there on the weekends and every other holiday. But it was so painfully obvious that we were the *other* kids, the *other* family. We were an inconvenience. We were the mistake he had to deal with now that he'd finally found his real life."

I understand how it feels when your parent lets you down, and my heart aches for him. "I'm so sorry."

"By the time Collin was born, my relationship with his mother was already over. We were young, and we'd never been serious, but the first time I held him in my arms, his eyes locked on mine and I knew I couldn't do to him what my father had done to me and Elle. I promised myself *he* would be my family. Even if his mom and I weren't together. It didn't matter. I promised I would never make him feel like he was second best."

"You're a great dad, Nate. You'd never make him feel like that."

"It's hard enough to be a kid to celebrity parents. I won't pile that on too." His hair falls into his face as he drops his head. "Collin is the most important thing in my life. I can't give you more without taking something from him. I won't do that."

"I wish you'd quit making it seem like I'm asking for that." My voice breaks because we both know I want more than this. Need more. A home. A life. Babies.

"What happens if we don't end this, Hanna? You can't be my mistress for the rest of my life. You can't keep flying out here when I snap my fingers." His face twists in disgust, and he steps away from me and into the rain. "Every time I say goodbye, I tell myself that's it. That I'll end it. Because you deserve that. But I'm weak and selfish as shit and keep calling you back because I can't get enough of you."

"What are you trying to say?"

He tilts his head to the sky and closes his eyes, letting the rain shower down on his face. I study the ridges of his strong back expanding as he breathes in and out.

I step into the rain and press my lips to the damp skin of his bare shoulder.

When he speaks, his question is so quietly murmured I can barely make it out over the rain in my ears. "Are you still in love with him?"

It's my turn to tense. "I am." I latch on to the best of my bravery and whisper, "But I'm in love with you too."

"Don't say that."

I back away. Slowly at first and then fast. Then I'm turning and running. Back into the house, up the stairs.

I crawl under the covers still in my rain-dampened robe and curl into a ball on my side.

When I hear him pad into the room, I don't roll over to look at him. When I feel the bed shift under his weight, I don't open my eyes. And when his arms wrap around me from behind and he pulls me to his chest, I don't say a word.

"I was in such an ugly, dark place the night we met. I looked into your eyes, and you were right there with me—my angel in the darkness. You saved me." He buries his nose in my hair and inhales audibly. "You saved me and I love you."

I draw in a gulp of air, but it enters my lungs with a sharp, painful edge.

"I think I've been in love with you since the night we met.

And I know that sounds crazy and implausible—like one of those things the guy says when he's trying to win the girl—but for me, it's just true. I love you and I'm terrified that you're going to ruin your life because of it." His arms tighten around me and he presses a kiss to my shoulder. "I'm not telling you to take his ring. I honestly believe that if he were worthy of you, you wouldn't be here with me. But don't let *me* be the reason you don't take the life you want."

"What if *you're* the life I want?"

His arms tighten around me and he presses his lips to my shoulder. "You're asking me for something I can't give."

Present Day

Nate's sitting on the edge of the big bed, elbows on his knees, studying the floor.

Rubbing sleep from my eyes, I push myself up and lean against the headboard. Next to me on the nightstand, my engagement ring stares back at me. I took it off last night. I should have left it at home. Ignoring it, I grab my phone to check the time. There's another message.

Nix: *Please call me soon!*

"I'm sorry. I'll get dressed and get out of here." I scramble to the edge of the bed.

He stops me with a hand on my wrist. "Are you going to be okay?"

"Yeah." I nod, trying for chipper, but I don't feel it. "I'll be fine."

"You took off the ring." He massages the back of his neck. "It's over?"

"It needs to be. I don't know how I'm supposed to move forward when what we have behind us hurts so much."

He studies me, his eyes full of thoughts I can't read and know he won't share. "You can stay here as long as you want. Take some time. Think things through. Jamaal will be here. He'll get you anything you need."

I tuck my feet under me and sit next to him. He's already dressed in dark jeans and a white button-up dress shirt. "Are you going somewhere?"

"I leave for Afghanistan this morning."

A memory flickers. "You're performing for the troops?"

"Yeah."

"How long until you leave?"

He cuts his eyes to me and pushes off the bed. "My driver's waiting out front."

"Is this it? Is this…goodbye? For good?"

He closes his eyes. "It has to be. "

I slide off the bed and touch my hand to his face. "How am I supposed to let you go?" I run my fingers along his jaw. "It's the right thing to do, but—" My voice breaks.

He cups my jaw, his fingers sliding into my hair. "I know your memory isn't the greatest right now," he says. "So I'm going to tell you the things I need you to remember for me."

"Okay."

"You are the most beautiful woman I have ever met." He swallows and braves a tentative smile. "You're like the sun— completely blind to your own beauty because you are so busy making everyone around you shine. No matter how far we hide in the shadows, you share your light. That's how you stole my heart when no one else could find it."

It hurts to breathe. "Nate."

Steps sound outside the heavy bedroom doors. "The plane's waiting, Crane." Jamaal's voice. "Time to head out."

Nate ignores him and keeps his dark eyes locked on mine.

"You have to go."

He holds me tight. "One more thing."

"What?" I don't know if I can handle anything else.

"Thank you," he whispers. "Thank you for giving something I never thought I deserved. And for giving it without expectation or condition. You made me believe I was worth it."

I shake my head, unsure of this metaphor. "My light?"

"Your love." He drops his hands and steps back.

I gulp in air and watch him back toward the door. Turn the knob. Walk away.

When he shuts the door behind him, I race to the bathroom, turning on the shower full blast because I can't stand the idea of letting him hear me cry.

I bite my fist to block the sobs, but they come anyway—thick and angry, ugly sobs of grief and self-pity. Because I don't have to know anything else about Nate Crane to know I love him. And he just said goodbye.

When the mirror is obscured by steam, I peel off my sleep clothes and step under the spray, letting it pound against me. I close my eyes and imagine the water can wash away all my heartache, all my fears and confusion. I lean my head against the glass enclosure and let the tears come.

My body rocks with my sobs. They tear out of me like my body rejecting poison. I let them come, and I let the water wash them away until my breathing evens and my tears are gone.

I don't know I'm not alone until hot, rough hands are on my bare shoulders, and Nate is turning me around.

"Nate," I breathe.

He's fully clothed, the water streaming down his face as he looks at me. "Why'd you have to forget?" Then his mouth is on mine, lips and tongue and teeth, taking and demanding and punishing.

I want this kiss too much to do anything but return it in kind. I suck at his lower lip and explore his mouth with my tongue. His taste is new and familiar all at once.

My hands go into his hair and I hold him close. I'm afraid he might disappear—that this might prove to be a hallucination—but he's solid under my hands. Water pours over us as we devour each other's mouths, and my hands find their way from his hair to his shoulders, his chest, and finally down to the hem of his shirt.

His mouth leaves mine just long enough for him to pull his shirt over his head and throw it to the shower floor. Then he's stepping into me again. One leg between my thighs, he presses me against the wall as his mouth returns to mine.

His kiss is softer this time. Slower, sweeter, and less desperate. If he was feasting on me before, now he's savoring me, and I let him. I savor him in return. The last sips of a precious bottle of wine, the last moments of a fleeting dream.

I don't know what I'm doing. I don't know what this means for tomorrow or next week. Right now, I don't care. I just need his hands on me, his taste on my tongue. I blindly grope for the button on his jeans. Releasing it, I shove them down his hips, and he kicks them away.

His hands grip my hips and he slides my body up the glass until my feet are off the ground and I'm resting on his thigh. The pressure is so perfect and so sweet. He rips his mouth from mine and moves to my neck as a hand cups my breast. I'm a mess of sensation and I don't want it to end—the press of his thigh between my legs, the tease of his thumb against my nipple, the scrape of his mouth against my neck.

"I've missed this," he murmurs.

Leaning my head back, I give up and let my eyes float shut. "What have you missed?"

"No, Hanna," he growls. "Look at me. I want you to remember who's touching you."

I force my eyes open and am treated to the sight of his head dipping to my breast. "Oh God." I should stop him. I shouldn't let it go this far. We both know what this is. A stolen moment. An extended goodbye. But his teeth scrape my nipple, and instead of protesting, I'm arching into his mouth, urging him on.

He squeezes my breast and groans as he lifts his head and returns his eyes to mine. He flicks my earlobe with his tongue. "I've missed your taste." He pinches my nipple between his fingers. "The way you cry out when I touch you." He repositions me between himself and the wall until my thighs cradle the bulge of his erection. "I missed the heat of your pussy when you're turned on."

Then his mouth is on mine again, his hands tangling in my wet hair as he devours me.

"The plane?"

"It's mine. It can wait."

Eventually, we make our way out of the shower and dry each other with fluffy white towels. Then he takes my hand and leads me to his bedroom. He slides under the covers with me. The frantic pace of the shower is gone and in its place is the steady beat of a grief-filled love song. He traces every line of my body with his fingers then his tongue. Love and need fill me so completely they hold together the pieces of my broken heart.

When Nate settles his head by mine on the pillow, his eyes are as tender as they are hot. "I have to let you go," he whispers. "This has to be goodbye."

My throat grows tight. "I know."

Chapter
TWENTY

FELL ASLEEP in his arms.

When I wake up again, the room is quiet. Nate is gone, his absence nearly tangible.

The covers smell like him. I can still feel the scrape of his beard against my skin. And despite this grief that makes my limbs feel heavy and my eyes gritty, I feel a sense of peace I haven't in weeks.

I climb out of bed and pull on a robe before padding down the stairs and out to the patio. The sun is high in the sky, warming the air and reflecting off the surface of the pool. Crystal sun catchers hang from the awning and spin in the breeze, casting dapples of light into the shadows by the door.

I close my eyes and step into the sun, letting the light warm my cheeks.

Inhale. Exhale. Let go.

I'm going to be okay.

My head is clear, the fog of the last two days lifted. And with my clarity comes the understanding. I wish I could've had more time with Nate, yet I'm glad he had to go. He needed me to let him go. We needed to let go of each other. Holding on to him was hurting him as much as it was hurting me.

And Max...

I open my eyes and tilt my face to the sky. Fluffy white clouds roll across the endless sea of blue.

I can forgive Max. I love him too much to hold on to my anger. I can forgive him. But I can't marry him. Maybe that will change with time, but I'm not going to ask him to live in limbo for me again. I have to let Max go too.

Canceling the wedding will break my mom's heart, but I need to make this decision for myself, not her. And regardless of what I may have been thinking when I put on Max's ring before my accident, regardless of what emotions or revelations I can't remember, I'm not ready to get married. Not to Max. Not to anyone. I'm still figuring out who I am and where I fit into my world.

I'm giving myself the gift of time and no attachments. Maybe my memories will return or maybe they won't. But whatever secrets are lost in my damaged brain, I've let the person I am—the person I want to become—get lost there too. Or maybe she was lost before my memories were. Maybe I lost myself three months ago when my world spiraled out of control.

I need to call Liz and make arrangements for a flight home. I need to call Max and my mom. Suddenly, calls that terrified me twenty-four hours ago are simply steps on a new path.

I climb the stairs back to Janelle's room. My phone flashes wildly at me from the nightstand, and I pick it up and open the latest text message.

Nix: *Call me. Now.*

I straighten. What if something happened to Liz? I hit the button to call her, and as it rings, I imagine half a dozen different scenarios in which Liz or Cally or my mom could have gotten hurt.

Suddenly, my stomach clenches and the peace I was feeling moments ago flees. What if something happened to Max? What if he's in the hospital and thinks I don't care? I flinch as guilt punches me in the gut.

"Come on, Nix," I whisper against the ring.

I'm expecting her voicemail when she finally picks up.

"Hanna!"

"Is everything okay?"

"Your blood work is back."

My shoulders sag in relief. No one is hurt. Nothing horrible has happened. Nix is just being doctor-ish. "Okay? Are my electrolytes still screwed up?"

"Your electrolytes are fine, but your hCG levels are elevated."

"What does that mean?"

"It means you're pregnant."

THE END

ACKNOWLEDGEMENTS

So many people help me bring a book together and this was no exception.

First, my husband, Brian, who never complains when date nights turn into brainstorming sessions and who is more than happy to tell me how he'd react to the drama I throw at my heroes. You, my love, are the real hero. Thanks for being awesome. I might keep you around after all.

To the medical professionals who helped me understand Hanna's condition and hospital protocol. To my sisters, Deb and Kim, and my mom—thank you for fielding my endless questions. Extra thanks to Eileen Dreyer, who didn't know me from Adam but happily answered my emails quizzing her about retrograde amnesia and dozens of what-ifs. These ladies provided me with more information than I could possibly include, steered me clear of plot holes, and inspired plot twists with their knowledge. Any errors are my own.

A huge thank you to my friends and family for being amazing cheerleaders. A special shout out to the "Indy Crew." I miss you guys and am so grateful to have your on-going support, virtual or otherwise. Justin, thanks for taking my plot question phone call while registering for your wedding gifts. That's above and beyond, sir.

To everyone who provided me feedback on this crazy twisty-turny plot—especially Violet Duke, Adrienne Hogan, and Annie Swanberg. Rock stars, all of you.

Thank you to the team that helped me package this book and promote it. Sarah Hansen at Okay Creations designed my beautiful cover, and if I have my way she will do many, many more for me. To my editing team, Rhonda Helms, Mickey Reed, and Arran Nicol, you make my books better. To Chris, my assistant, who keeps me organized against all odds. A massive shout-out to Julie with ATOMR for organizing my promotional events and to all of the bloggers and reviewers who help spread the word about my books. Amazing. Every one of you.

To my agent Dan Mandel and my foreign rights agent Stefanie Diaz for getting my books into the hands of readers all over the world—you're making my dreams come true.

To all my writer friends on Twitter, Facebook, and my various writer loops, thank you for your support and inspiration. Special thanks to the NWB—Sawyer Bennett, Lauren Blakely, Violet Duke, Jessie Evans, Melody Grace, Monica Murphy, and Kendall Ryan—you ladies make me smile on a daily basis!

And last but certainly not least, thank you to my fans all over the world. To those who read *Unbreak Me* and *Wish I May* and wrote begging for another New Hope story. To those who follow me on Facebook and tell me to write faster because you can't wait. You're the best fans an author could ask for. I couldn't do this without you and wouldn't want to. Thank you for buying my books and telling your friends about them. Thank you for asking me to write more. You're the best!

~Lexi

Lost In Me Playlist

Anna Nalick—*Breathe (2am)*
Barenaked Ladies—*Odds Are*
Dave Matthews Band—*The Space Between*
Matchbox Twenty—*If You're Gone*
Shakira, Rihanna—*Can't Remember to Forget You*
Sarah Bareilles—*I Choose You*
Jason Mraz—*I Won't Give Up*
Nine Inch Nails—*Something I Can Never Have*
A Great Big World—*Say Something*
P.M. Dawn—*I'd Die Without You*
Jason Walker—*Down*
Macy Gray—*I Try*
James Blunt—*You're Beautiful*

Other Titles
by LEXI RYAN

New Hope Series
Unbreak Me
Stolen Wishes
Wish I May

Hot Contemporary Romance
Text Appeal
Accidental Sex Goddess

Stiletto Girls Novels
Stilettos, Inc.
Flirting with Fate

Decadence Creek
Just One Night
Just the Way You Are

Excerpts from Lauren Blakely and Rhonda Helms

I'm excited to share my release day with two talented writers and friends. I've included snippets of their new releases for you below.

About *First Night*
An erotic novella from the *New York Times* and *USA Today* Bestselling author Lauren Blakely...

It was only supposed to be one night...

When the sinfully handsome man walks into her bar in San Francisco, Julia Bell simply wants a break from the troubles that keep chasing her. That escape comes in the form of sexy, confident and commanding Clay Nichols, who captivates her mind AND turns her inside out with pleasure. The attraction is electric and they share one scorchingly hot night together, but they also discover there is more than just off-the-charts chemistry; the connection between them runs deep. Clay never thought he'd return to New York with this woman still on his mind. But he can't get her out of his system, and he needs more of her...He wants more than just the first night...

This is a prequel novella to the erotic romance NIGHT AFTER NIGHT.

Excerpt of *First Night* © Lauren Blakely

"We have an India Pale Ale tonight. Will that do?"

"That'll do just fine," he said, his muscular forearms resting on the sleek bar. His shirt sleeves were rolled up and Julia couldn't help but notice how strong his arms were. She bet he worked out. A real man kind of workout. Something hard and heavy that made him sweat and grunt to mold that kind of physique. She poured the beer into the glass, and set it down in front of him. He reached for his wallet, peeled off some bills, and handed them to her.

"I take it you're Julia?"

Uh oh. How did he know her name. Was he an undercover cop? Had she accidentally served someone under twenty-one? She was diligent and methodical in her ID checking and had never let an underage in. Or wait. Her spine stiffened. Was he onto her? Did he know what she did every Tuesday night at a dimly-lit apartment above a greasy restaurant in ChinaTown that smelled of fried pork? That would be over soon though. It had to be. She'd done her time, and was ready to cash in. Soon, she kept telling herself.

"Yeah," she answered carefully, all her senses on alert. She wasn't really doing anything wrong those nights, was she? No, she was just taking care of business as she knew how.

"I hear you're the best bartender in San Francisco."

The tightness in her shoulders relaxed. At least he wasn't a boy in blue come to bust her. But forget his smoldering looks. He was like the rest of them, going for cheap lines, hitting on the woman behind the bar. "Yeah, where'd you hear that? Facebook?"

He smiled briefly, shook his head. Damn, he had a fabulous smile. Straight, white teeth and a knowing grin. But she knew better than to fall for a hot stranger simply because he was handsome. She'd done that before, and it had kicked her in the ass. That's why she was a No-Strings-Attached kind of woman these days. Not that she'd had any attachments of any sort lately – she had too much trouble to untangle herself from before she could even think about getting tangled up in love, let alone the sheets.

"No. Your sister told me. McKenna, I believe."

Oh.

Oh yes.

It all made sense now.

And far be it from Julia to ever doubt her big sister. Because McKenna's assessment was one hundred and fifty percent correct. He was smoking hot. Un-be-lievable. And he was no longer a stranger. He was sister-approved, he wasn't a copy, and he wasn't a heavy, so she shucked off her worries. "Clay Nichols," he said, offering a hand to shake. Nice firm grip. Before she knew it, she was thinking of other uses for those strong hands.

About *One Broke Girl* **by Rhonda Helms**

Anna Parker's life disintegrates with one phone call. Her dad's selling their ritzy New York City condo because her Wall Street banker mom emptied their bank account and ran off with another man. Which means Anna has to drop out of her elite college and move with Dad back to their small Ohio hometown. Anna's determined to reclaim her life ASAP, so she'll use the next few months to save money, help Dad get back on his feet, and find and confront her mom.

But Anna doesn't anticipate things going so wrong. The only job she can get is working as a lunch lady in an elementary school. Their money-pit duplex is falling apart around their feet. And her dad is depressed without her mom, who's proving hard to find.

One bright spot in the chaos is Gavin Metcalf, a kindergarten teacher she dated when they were young teens. With his easy wit and sexy smiles, he makes her forget her stresses—and the fact that her boyfriend Steven back in New York doesn't know the truth yet about her dire circumstances. When past and present collide, Anna has to decide where her future lies...

Excerpt of *One Broke Girl* © **Rhonda Helms**

The song pouring through the speakers changed to a deep, throbbing bass, and the crowd's mood shifted into a sensual vibe.

"Will you dance with me?" Gavin asked in a sexy tone that made my belly flutter.

I should say no, because I was beyond attracted to this guy, despite my efforts. But I found myself starting to sway. He didn't touch me, just let the inches of space between us thicken with tension. We moved in silence, eyes locked in an intensity I'd never experienced before. It was like he could see inside me, knew the inappropriate thoughts I was having.

I was so turned on, even as I fought against it.

All too soon, the song ended. With heated eyes, Gavin brushed his fingers along my forearm, then turned and walked off the dance floor.

"Wow," Bianca said as she joined me, tugging Natalie's hand to draw her into our circle. "That was hot. I almost had an O just watching you two."

I barked out a laugh as my face flamed. I said to them both in a casual tone, "Oh, he apologized for being a jerk earlier. It was nice of him to do so when he didn't have to. And he asked me to be his friend, too, which I think is great. Everyone could use more friends, right?" My excuses were paper-thin, a barfing of words, but they were all I had right now, so I clung to them.

Bianca's grin widened. "Girl, if that's friendship, I'm obviously making the wrong kind of friends."

Contact
LEXI RYAN

I love hearing from readers, so find me on my Facebook page at facebook.com/lexiryanauthor, follow me on Twitter @ writerlexiryan, shoot me an email at writerlexiryan@gmail.com, or find me on my website: www.lexiryan.com

This paperback interior was designed and formatted by

www.emtippettsbookdesigns.com

Artisan interiors for discerning authors and publishers.

Made in the USA
Lexington, KY
18 June 2014